Pathway to Murder

A crime-fiction mystery

by

G.D. Northcott

First published in Great Britain by Pen Press

All paper used in the printing of this book has been made from
wood grown in managed, sustainable forests.

ISBN13: 978-1-78003-357-0

Printed and bound in the UK
Pen Press is an imprint of
Indepenpress Publishing Limited
25 Eastern Place
Brighton
BN2 1GJ

A catalogue record of this book is available from
the British Library

From the author of *The Traveller's Companion*.

There has to be a twist.

CONTENTS

CHAPTER ONE

OPEN VERDICT

Independently minded Constance York, living on her own, died a swift but agonising death in her own bed at her apartment in Orange Tree Court, Croydon. The door and windows were fastened, a task she undertook every night before turning in. The post-mortem revealed chemical burning of her intestine, but no burning to the lips or throat. Traces of a glutinous substance were found by the autopsy, which led the report to conclude that poison had been administered in capsule form. A glass by the bedside contained water only. No matching toxin was found in or on anything in the flat. Photographs, fingerprints and other customary procedures were completed with the usual efficiency.

The options considered by the police were:

Suicide: there was no note left by her to make things simple for them.

Accidental: a most unlikely scenario.

Intentional: pointed strongly in that direction, but who was responsible?

The dark-haired Constance York had been seen entering the building on her own at roughly six o'clock by the caretaker, and had not been seen to leave for the rest of the evening. No visitors had been noticed for certain calling on her after she had arrived home.

Only the one bottle that contained the capsules was found. According to the label they were for an allergy complaint. The remaining capsules were sent for analysis. The contents were as marked on the label, which showed that the gelatine type was identical to that found in the stomach of the deceased. The only fingerprints on the bottle and glass of water were those of Constance York. The capsules had a popular brand name and could be bought over the counter at most chemists'. The elongated capsules could be pulled apart in two halves and pushed together again quite easily. Each one contained granules of various sizes. Some dissolved quickly, others taking longer, claiming to give the sufferer continuous relief.

The police endeavoured to get in touch with her associates, family, those she might have socialised with and anyone they could find who had spoken to her on that fateful day. What sort of person was she, had anyone a grudge strong enough to want her dead, and of course they needed to establish the motive and opportunity. She had been married for about eight years. The relationship had ended in divorce some two and a half years earlier. Her only living relative was a brother who lived and worked abroad.

Fingerprints, as one would expect, were everywhere, mostly smudged. In the bedroom three were legible: Constance York's and two others. The second set turned out to be those of the cleaning lady, who agreed for them to be taken and compared. The third, a single print, was not on criminal records and therefore remained unidentified.

The company making and distributing the capsules were contacted. Their strict method of packaging appeared to rule out accidental or deliberate inclusion of poison in their product at source. At the coroner's inquest, it was known where, when and how. Natural or accidental cause of death was ruled out. The finding was an open verdict with probable criminal intent, by a person or persons unknown.

With so little to go on, the police soon found themselves at a dead end. The investigation notes of that case were placed in the Unsolved Crime file.

Two weeks before Constance York's death, the wealthy political figure Lord Peter Fairfield was working in his study at his luxurious country home in Oakwood, organising business and parliamentary affairs. The phone rang. Peter lifted the receiver. A voice said in a soft, deep tone, 'I've just found out some disturbing information. If it became public knowledge it could easily cause you a great deal of embarrassment.'

Peter was taken aback for a moment or two. 'Information... what sort of information?' Then he asked bluntly, 'Who the devil are you?'

The caller hesitated for a while, then in a cautious voice said, 'That's unimportant for now. I'm not sure whether this is the right time.'

Peter, becoming impatient, said irritably, 'Go to hell, whoever you are!' and replaced the receiver with annoyed force. Peter had had a challenging week, and this was the last straw.

When his son Phillip paid him a visit, Peter carelessly mentioned the phone call and what little had been said, believing it would go no further. He was wrong.

'One of your lady friends, going to spill the beans on you,' Phillip said.

'Utter nonsense, Phil. How could you say such a thing?'

'That's as may be, Dad, but you have a reputation of having an eye for the ladies, according to some of your so-called friends I've spoken to.'

'They can say what they jolly well like. Most of them are not so innocent themselves. Hopeless hypocrites, who are they to talk?' Peter emphasised. 'Damn the lot of them. I can't wait to get away for a while. And, by the way, I'm giving the staff here time off as well.'

'That's rather generous of you. Who's going to look after the place?'

'Not really; they'll be going the day after I leave and be back the day before I return. My work will be up to date, and no one needs to be here while I'm away. I can't remember the last time I gave myself a complete break.'

Phillip did not keep to himself what his father had told him, and did not treat it as confidential. He spoke of what had been said to his wife. Once she'd heard, it quickly became known to others. As word passed along, it sounded more sinister, threatening that something damaging to the family name would be revealed at a later date. Were there skeletons in Peter's cupboard, his brother in particular considered, that he hadn't already known about?

The day came for Peter Fairfield to depart from Oakwood for his long overdue break. Leaving the manor by car, he felt momentarily that prying eyes were on him – or was that only his imagination? And yet – there was a car with a young woman not far from the entrance. He looked back; she wasn't following.

Arriving at Gatwick airport, he went straight to the check-in desk and deposited his suitcases. After making his way through security into the departure lounge, he sat and waited comfortably for his gate number to come up on the monitor screen. When eventually this was given, he proceeded to the gate-numbered lounge, awaiting the call to be given for boarding the aircraft. An elderly military-looking gentleman sat next to him. The two chatted until the call came to board the plane. After a few hours the aircraft arrived and landed safely but precariously at Corfu airport. There were no prying eyes here, he felt.

Some people were waiting outside the exit doors for passengers on the incoming flights. A man held up to his chest a card with Peter's name written on it. Making his way over to the man, Peter identified himself as the one being paged.

'You English, yes, ah, I take you Kassiopi... you will like. My car, he is outside. It will be bumpy ride, sorry – many potholes in road – bends winding, very narrow. No space for buses passing, must hold back... and big drop in places—'

Peter raised his eyebrows. 'Are you always so damned cheerful?'

The driver laughed. 'I tell you something else, my friend, it is not now allowed to smoke on the public transport... and if you are sick on a coach, you will be fined much money.'

'I'll bear that in mind,' Peter said.

The journey in his taxi through old Corfu town itself was not as Peter had expected it to be. It appeared to him to be shabby and neglected. The beauty of the island became apparent once they were out of town and travelling along the rugged coast road. What struck him in particular was the slow, easy going pace of life, compared to the rush and bustle of England. On the way to Kassiopi they occasionally passed an old man or old woman riding a donkey.

The fishing village of Kassiopi with its little harbour was quaint. Small boats were anchored, men leisurely mending their nets. There were pleasure boats that catered for tourists, for day trips and beach barbecues. All around the harbour were tavernas, where one could enjoy the best of Greek food and wines.

The villas and apartments built on the land surrounding the harbour were not allowed to spoil or overpower the charm of the place. The buildings were restricted in height by the authorities; there were no high rise buildings at all.

The taxi travelled close by a narrowing street towards the harbour. An old man was sweeping up litter with a birch broom that appeared to be a size too big for him, shovelling the rubbish into what looked like two dustbins on a handcart. Peter observed it was gone eight o'clock in the evening, their time. It was unusual to see workmen out and about this late, but then, this was Corfu. Gift shops, places to eat and grocery stores lay back on both sides of the street.

The taxi turned sharply to go uphill to a small, secluded private villa; here was where he would be away from his demanding relations, do what he liked and unwind for a time, away from prying eyes and questions.

Oakwood, where he lived, was also a charming quiet village, with an inn aptly named Fourways because of the four roads leading in different directions on which one could choose to travel when leaving the place. Fourways was a cosy country inn; a wood fire burned and crackled in the grate in cold weather. Here one could stay and be served country cheeses, crispy baked bread and succulent ham carved from the bone. Mouth-watering when washed down with true old English ale to complete the pleasure. Many local homemade wines were available, along with other 'pub grub' meals.

Peter enjoyed every day of his stay on the island, letting his hair down, doing things he could not be seen doing back in England.

The morning Peter Fairfield left for the airport for his flight home, the cleaners came to the villa. They were hard at work when one of them found something between a cushion and the back of the settee. She put her fingers deep down and retrieved what she thought at first to be a cigarette lighter. It turned out to be a tube of lipstick. There were other tell-tale signs of female company. She cheekily grinned. Holding up what she had found, she said to the others, 'Well, now, our distinguished holiday-maker has not been lonely while staying here... now has he?'

CHAPTER TWO

FRIDAY'S GATHERING

They began to arrive at Fairfield Manor. The first member of the family was Edgar Fairfield – Lord Peter Fairfield's brother. A stocky man with a round jovial face, completely bald from the forehead through the centre to the crown of his head. As he lived barely five miles away from the manor, a few recent documents of importance had been entrusted to him for safe keeping before his brother's departure to Corfu. He was now glad that he would be returning them to him on Sunday.

John French greeted Edgar in front of the house. John, a meticulous man, organised almost everything for his employer, Peter Fairfield. The small number of staff at the manor consisted of Emily Spake, the housekeeper, a methodical woman, one inch less than five feet in height; her husband Wally, gardener and chauffeur, also capable of doing the odd job after a predictable moan and groan; the cook, Molly Ebson, a widow, and her two teenage daughters, Elsie and Freda, both serving as maids and on general domestic chores at the manor. All five were given paid leave for the short time Peter Fairfield was away. These free days from everyday chores suited the Ebsons and Emily Spake, but Wally was none too pleased. He was a habitual groaner but with a heart of gold.

'Our family get-togethers can be mercilessly irritating,' Edgar said to John French as the two men unloaded a few items from the boot of John's car. If Edgar expected a response, it never came; the other man's thoughts were elsewhere.

Next to make an appearance was Phillip Fairfield, the eldest son, accompanied by his self-opinionated wife, Angela. Phillip had a small, thin moustache that looked out of place. Then came the unpredictable Donald Fairfield, with his down-to-earth, quietly spoken wife, Elizabeth. Last on the scene were Peter's attractive daughter Pamela Fairfield and her work colleague Basil Broadwater. Pamela had known Basil for some considerable time; they attended the same art classes and both now worked for a firm noted for its expertise in the restoration of paintings. Disingenuous Basil strongly fancied his chances of marrying into the Fairfield family. He was good-looking, tall, slim and full of false charm, switched on at will whenever he felt it would benefit him.

After settling in, the party met up for drinks in the sitting-room.

Phillip stood with his back to the fire, warming his posterior and puffing at a cigar. He looked mischievously at the small group gathered in front of him. 'Nice to see the family get together, and for the return of our happy wanderer,' he said. 'Frenchy here doing all the graft as usual.'

'Don't call him Frenchy,' Pamela said. 'He's not keen on being called that.'

'I knew someone once who came from Yorkshire. At the office, they called him Yorky for short,' Elizabeth told them amiably.

'Nonsense, Liz – that would mean John here came from France,' remarked Donald smugly.

'Your trouble is you think you know it all, and you don't. Get off your high horse,' Elizabeth said disapprovingly.

Donald wasn't listening.

'How are you keeping Uncle Edgar? And how is Aunt Harriet?' Phillip asked him.

'Harriet's no better but I'm fine, apart from being a bit humiliated yesterday.'

All eyes turned on him.

'What do you mean, humiliated?' asked Elizabeth.

'I was queuing up at the post office; there was a woman in front of me and another behind me with a large dog on a long lead. The dog edged in front of me and rubbed its nose on the woman's bottom. She swung round and accused me. I thought she was about to slap my face. I said "nothing to do with me" and pointed to the dog. We laughed afterwards but I felt so small.'

'Serves you right, blaming the dog,' said Angela.

'Somehow, I expected that remark from you,' replied Edgar in an injured tone of voice.

John French felt out of place, and said, 'As arranged, Wally will collect Peter from the airport in the morning. Now... I hope there's nothing more, and that you all have a pleasant weekend. I'll make my way home... it's been a long day.'

'Just one thing,' Angela responded. 'Everything's been all right with Peter, has it? No more indiscretions to damage the family name. I hope you've not heard of the old fool misbehaving whilst he's been away.'

'I can't believe my ears! You may not mean it, but you have a perverted sense of humour, with a guest and an employee here,' reacted Pamela. She had nothing but contempt for Angela. There was no love lost between them. She also despised Phillip at that moment for saying nothing in his father's defence. After all, he was a prominent figure and no fool.

Basil Broadwater looked down at his drink, not getting involved.

Angela was amused. 'Who rattled your cage? John's more like a friend of the family, you know that… and as for Basil, well, he's practically part of it, dear, isn't he?' she mocked.

'Basil's only a colleague, as well you know,' Pamela answered irritably.

It's just a matter of time before I win her over, Basil felt.

'Angela's never been a one for diplomacy,' admitted Phillip, unashamed.

John French felt awkward and fidgeted. He looked directly at Angela, saying, 'When Peter returns you can ask him about your concern. I really must be going.'

'There's no point in me remaining,' said Edgar. 'I'll be popping in on Peter sometime on Sunday.'

As a friendly gesture, Phillip said, 'What shall we all get up to this evening? Anyone for a four at cards? I wouldn't mind a game.'

'I'd like to be one,' Basil said keenly.

'Count me in,' said Angela, unremorseful for her earlier tomfoolery.

'If there's no objection from Pam and my dear husband,' Liz said sarcastically, 'I'll make the fourth.'

Pamela smiled at her. 'You go ahead, no cards for me. There's an art programme I want to watch.'

'You carry on. I've brought a book on wines I'm keen to read,' Donald said.

Edgar hurried his drink. 'I'll walk you as far as your car, John.'

The private secretary and Edgar were escorted to the front door by Donald. 'Goodnight, Edgar; give my regards to Auntie… and, John, thank you for your help and hard work. The household would be lost without you.'

John gratefully acknowledged the encouraging words, taking them with a pinch of salt. 'Thank you, Donald; nice to know someone's appreciative. Kindly give my regards to your father. I'll see him in Westminster as we arranged over the phone.' He was pleased at last to have finished ministering to their needs and unpredictable ways.

John led the way, quickening his pace. The cool night air made them both shudder a little as they left the warmer temperature of the house behind them.

'Brrr, what a difference out here,' remarked Edgar. 'It's a bit chilly for this time of the year – where is your car now?'

'Wind blowing from the northeast,' said John. 'I've moved down by the small gate. Don't bother coming; you'll only have to walk back to your own.'

'With my physique, the exercise will do me good. That odd phone call Peter had, it couldn't be anything to do with money; he's quite well off,' he said enviously. 'Any other misdemeanour on his part would be equally ludicrous to imagine – apart from womanising.'

'Sorry, Edgar, I'm not interested in your brother's private life; it's really nothing to do with me. Angela speaking like she did was out of order. I will say this in Peter's defence: he told Phillip everything, being quite open about it all, pooh-poohing the idea. It might have been better to have heard what the caller had to say without hanging up. That might have put an end to it. Whoever it was could have dialled the wrong number even, by mistake; who knows? Why make nasty remarks in front of everybody? Pamela was quite annoyed with Angela and Phillip – couldn't help but notice. Better to have kept a phone call like that to himself.' He paused. 'Peter's logic of late is puzzling. He said before he left that he wanted a complete rest and change of scenery, and what did he do? Started writing another political paper, so he tells me over the phone. The sad thing about politics and this incompetent government is that they don't know they are incompetent.'

'Politics bore me, but that could be his way of relaxing,' suggested Edgar.

'He could have done that just as easily at home.

'Hopefully we'll hear no more said of that stupid call.'

'I'll drink to that.'

At that point, they reached John French's car. After farewells, Edgar returned to his own car and drove off in the opposite direction.

Back at the house, Pamela was briefly discussing the forthcoming weekend with Basil. She avoided Angela as best she could; they never really hit it off. Things had not changed for the better even after becoming sisters-in-law. Angela made no pretence of her great pleasure in goading Pamela; the more she took the bait, the more she was teased. Elizabeth on the other hand was not in the market for scoring points from either one of them, and was regarded by Angela as no adversary, giving her the impression of a 'dizzy blonde', muddled and inoffensive. But not half-witted, as she was proving to Angela at the card table. The two women were playing a few hands until being joined by their card partners. Phillip and Donald were engaged in glum conversation, by the look on their stern faces, as if discussing something of national importance. Only for it to be nothing more than their business activities. Phillip dabbled in property development and Donald in the importation of wines.

It was customary for members of the family to spend weekends at the manor. It was, however, unusual for them all to be there at the same time. Lord Fairfield played host to political as well as business associates with regularity, through the week as well as weekends. Just of late it had dropped off slightly. Pamela had lived there until work had required her to live nearer London. Fortunately her aunt had a house not far from Kew Gardens and had welcomed her to stay. This arrangement she found acceptable, allowing her to commute to the city without too much difficulty.

It was the third appearance at the manor for Basil Broadwater. Pamela believed that he'd no inkling of what the fuss was about. He'd put it down to Angela having had too much gin, she hoped.

The domestic staff had their rooms on the uppermost floor of the manor. Molly Ebson was saying to her daughters later that night, 'Fancy having all that shower descending on us down here, the first time he's back. No consideration at all for those that have to prepare meals and clean up after 'em.'

'Come off it, Mum,' Freda chimed in. 'We've had a break, paid for doing nothing. You want jam on it, you do.'

'It's not that bad; we have our slack times as well as busy ones. And in any case, I've missed seeing Arnold,' Elsie said. Her eyes held a mischievous sparkle. Arnold was a young lad who worked down on East Farm, only a stone's throw away from Oakwood.

'I should have known,' her mother said glumly, resigned to the fact that she wouldn't always have her girls with her.

In another room, Wally Spake was in a melancholy mood, sitting on a stool polishing his shoes in preparation for the following morning.

His wife looked at him thoughtfully.

'You're very quiet,' she said to him.

'I'm not back in the swing of things yet, Emily. I was thinking about all the garden jobs that's been neglected. Grass out back needs a chop. My ruddy fault. Out of sight – out of mind. I wouldn't be surprised to find lions and tigers roaming around in that jungle when I get around to cutting it.'

'Come off it, it's hardly had time to grow an inch the time we've been away. Think yourself lucky; you're never satisfied,' she said disapprovingly.

He brushed polish on his hand, cursed, and went on polishing. 'You could 'ave knocked me down with a feather when old Fairfield said, "'ave some days away on full pay." I said to 'im, "I'd prefer to stay, for personal reasons." He said, "You would?" I said, "I would." He said, "You sure?" I said, "I'm sure." It made no ruddy difference once he'd made up his mind.'

'Is the car spick and span?' Emily enquired.

'As clean as my shoes.' He looked them over with satisfaction and put them on the floor. 'Mind you, the old girl always coughs and splutters a bit... now ticks over like a Swiss watch. And your tasks?' he asked benevolently.

Emily removed spectacles from a determined nose. 'All done, everything in readiness for the return of His Nibs.'

'Don't you let old Fairfield hear you saying that,' said Wally jovially.

'You're a fine one to talk about being disrespectful, calling him old Fairfield,' retorted Emily, seeing the funny side. 'Talk about the pot calling the kettle black!'

Wally gave an exaggerated yawn 'Shut up, woman; you ready for bed? It's early to rise for me.'

CHAPTER THREE

RETURN HOME

It had begun to rain steadily in the early hours of Saturday morning, becoming heavier as the new day progressed. Wally Spake drove in silence, pushing his way slowly through the heavy rain to the airport. The wiper blades were at full speed and he strained his eyes with concentration on the thickening traffic as the car moved nearer to Gatwick. He reflected on why he'd taken the trouble to clean the car, and his ruddy shoes.

Reaching Gatwick, he made his way to the short-stay car park, from which, after parking, he took a lift to the arrival section. He glanced at his wristwatch to find that he had plenty of time for a cup of tea and a snack before flight 9021 was to land. Against his better judgment, and after a change of mind, he seated himself at a table-clothed table and tucked with relish into a belated cooked breakfast, followed by two cups of tea. Paying the bill at the cash-desk on the way out, he cursed under his breath, 'Bloody airport prices.'

The plane touched down one hour late. Wally suspected that the car park fees would be high when they left, reassuring himself that the money would be refunded by his employer. He spotted Lord Fairfield almost immediately as the crowd came ambling through the open doors from customs. Why do people amble through customs? he wondered. Is it because under watchful eyes one feels guilty, even when there's nothing to feel guilty about?

The crowd thinned and Wally saw his employer pushing an overloaded trolley. Lord Fairfield was first to speak. 'Hello, Wally, nice to see you again; thank you for coming.'

Wally grinned and thought, Didn't have much choice, I had to bloody come, saying simply, 'Hello, sir, welcome back. I trust you are well.'

'Mustn't grumble, mustn't grumble,' Fairfield replied, characteristically repeating himself. 'Home comforts basic on Corfu, but adequate.'

Peter Fairfield had an anaemic-looking face in spite of having been in a climate that should have given him a better colour. He was tall with a good crop of hair. Curiously enough, although he was pale, one fact was incontestable: he looked in good shape.

The return journey would take longer. The traffic was thicker than Wally had hoped for, but he was in no particular hurry and the rain had stopped.

Only when the car drove off the motorways and on to the quieter roads did Peter Fairfield become talkative again. 'Nothing amiss at the manor, no problems I hope,' he said calmly, and went on, 'This break has done me a power of good. I dare say you also enjoyed the short time off. We all need to recharge our batteries from time to time.'

'Yes, thank you, sir, we made good use of the time, Emily and me. All is well at the house. And yes, not only cars need a recharge. Too true we do.'

Peter Fairfield became silent again and with a notepad and pencil started to jot some things down: *House of Lords - a well worn subject. Most hereditary peers gave wise counsel, had expertise second to none and were excellent in debate. They have given countless years of incalculable service. Their roles at Westminster, and why the need for a second chamber. The desire for a more democratic system of replacing the privileged and, in the eyes of many, unacceptable hereditary system. What are the 'for' and 'against' to certain arguments; must leave the reader to form his or her own opinion.* And so on and so on, the jottings went on, until all of a sudden the car slowed, gently turned and went through the big gates of Fairfield Manor.

'There already!' Peter Fairfield said, surprised. 'I was miles away.'

'Here we are, sir, home again,' replied Wally.

As the car neared the front of the building, some of the family and staff came out to greet Peter. Wally let him out of the car, Peter not knowing then what the following months had in store for him. Wally then drove on to the garages around the back. Lord Fairfield's baggage and items he had purchased were still in the boot of the car. Wally moaned and groaned as he struggled to take them into the house through the back entrance.

CHAPTER FOUR

UNWELCOME CALLER

At the village police station in Burbridge the telephone rang. PC Timothy Myers answered. 'Burbridge police, how can I help?'

A policewoman at the other end said, 'This is New Scotland Yard; my chief inspector Reginald Morgan would like a word with Sergeant Porterdale.'

The constable put her on hold, then got through to his superior. 'I hope it's not a prank, but I have someone on hold from Scotland Yard – so they say.'

'Put 'em through, Tim.'

'Right, Sergeant.'

After the policewoman had Sergeant Porterdale on the line, she connected the chief inspector.

'Ah, Sergeant, good afternoon. My name is Morgan; I've been given your chief constable's blessing to contact you. I have a delicate job for you.'

'Yes, sir,' he answered with interest.

'This is just an inquiry, but needs to be handled with a touch of diplomacy. You see, it's like this: I have to speak to a Lord Peter Fairfield who lives in Oakwood, which is not far away from you there in Burbridge. As it is far better to have a personal call, rather than a phone call or anything written down, I'd like you to arrange a meeting for me to see him in private. He can either come to the Yard or I will visit him at his offices or home... whatever he prefers. I would like to emphasise that you are completely alone with him when you approach him on the subject.'

'May I ask the nature of the inquiry?'

'No, I'm afraid not... not at the moment. It's just routine. I don't want things blown out of all proportion when Scotland Yard start asking questions of someone with a title. Perhaps I'm being overcautious, but I ask you please not to mention my request to anyone.'

'You have my word, sir.'

'Good; now, will you call on him in plain clothes or uniform?'

'I don't think it really matters,' Porterdale answered casually. 'Some time ago we were officially requested to keep an eye on his place in his short absence. We were made aware of his departure and homecoming. I can go with the pretext of a courtesy call.'

'Good, do as you think fit. Ring me on extension 192 at the Yard when you've something for me.'

'How urgent is this?'

'Whenever you can swing it.'

'Right, sir, I'll get on to it as soon as possible.'

After the conversation ended, PC Myers could not wait to ask whether the call was genuine. He was politely told it was, and nothing more.

The sergeant gave little thought over the matter of calling at the manor in uniform. Police uniform or a vicar's dog-collar got you in places where ordinary clothing would not. If he wore plain clothes, it was likely they'd say, 'Have you an appointment?' or 'His Lordship is not seeing anyone today,' etcetera, etcetera.

It was late afternoon when Sergeant Porterdale arrived at the large oak door of the manor. He was well over six feet tall. Emily Spake looked up at him as she opened the door. Her expression showed surprise at seeing a policeman standing there in front of her.

'Yes?' she asked rather timidly.

He spoke with as much authority as he could muster: 'I'd be obliged if Lord Fairfield would give me a few moments of his time. I found myself in the vicinity and would like a word with regard to the safety of the property. We've been warned to be on our guard.'

'You'd better come in, then; I'll see if he's free.'

After guiding Porterdale into the study, the housekeeper closed the door behind her and went along to Lord Fairfield, who was in a reluctant conversation with Phillip and Angela. Lord Fairfield was saying, 'That's the problem with a lot of businesses: all they think of when the going's good is expand, expand, expand. When the market drops they're in trouble.'

'You'd be surprised at the drastic steps I've had to take to keep afloat,' Phillip said bitterly. 'It's not my fault, the state of the market.'

'I wouldn't in the least, knowing you. You should have been prudent enough to have kept your capital reserve in a healthy state and not squandered when the money was coming in thick and fast,' Lord Fairfield insisted. 'As you well know, the banks all over the world have done the same as you have and lost billions by their bad judgment.'

All three went quiet as Emily approached.

'Excuse me please, sorry to disturb you. There's a policeman wanting to know if you will see him, sir. He's waiting in the study.'

Phillip and Angela looked at one other with questioning eyes.

'What's it about, Emily? Did he say?'

'Yes, sir, something to do with security I think, checking to see if everything is as it should be, something like that.'

'If it had been otherwise, they'd have been the first to know,' Angela protested sourly. 'You ought to have known better, dear! Letting him in the house when Peter has company! You should have sent him on his way with a flea in his ear.'

Emily was taken aback and took umbrage. 'Madam,' she said strongly, 'decisions of that nature are not mine to make.'

Angela was barely listening and ignored the little woman's remark. She rose to her feet, twisted her lips and turned her attention to her father-in-law. 'Most inconsiderate; make him come back another time Peter, when it's more convenient. I think he's got a bit of a cheek calling without prior warning. There is so much we need to talk about. He's as welcome as a wasp on a nudist beach at the moment.'

'Or a pork pie in a synagogue,' Phillip added dryly, with a one-sided twisted smile.

Peter looked at them fretfully. He found Angela most tiresome in one of her domineering moods. Although she came from a good background, and felt superior, she was no lady. He turned to the housekeeper. 'Emily, tell him I'll join him in a few moments.'

When the housekeeper was out of earshot, Peter said, 'Really, Angela, you are most trying at times.' He walked away briskly.

All went quiet for a while, then Phillip said, 'I really can't see your logic; what's the big deal? Our business can wait. Why make so much fuss? We have to keep on the good side of Dad at the moment.'

Sergeant Porterdale stood admiring a painting that hung over the mantelpiece when Peter Fairfield entered the room.

'Good afternoon, Sergeant; your visit is untimely but you must have a reason.'

'I apologise for calling on the off chance, sir, but I was detailed to do so. My orders were to speak to you privately.'

'Can't be that important; nothing amiss with the premises, I assure you.'

'Actually, sir, that's not my reason for calling. I've been asked to come here personally by a Chief Inspector Reginald Morgan of Scotland Yard. He would like to see you, at your convenience, and speak with you in private. He has given me the job of making the arrangements for this. He felt it more appropriate for me to do so. You may call in at the Yard if you so wish, or he can call at your offices or home, whichever option is preferable to you.'

'Scotland Yard! In connection with what?'

'I'm sorry, sir, I've not been taken into their confidence and happy not to.' Porterdale felt he ought to have phrased that differently.

'One moment,' Peter said wonderingly, and consulted a tattered diary on his desk. 'Wednesday, this coming Wednesday, I'll be at home here all day. We will not be disturbed. Shall we say three o'clock? Can that be arranged?'

'I'm sure it can, sir; I'll confirm it, of course. Sorry once again for troubling you.'

Porterdale left inconspicuously and returned to Burbridge police station where he made the call to Scotland Yard, happy to have fulfilled his mission.

CHAPTER FIVE

FURTHER INQUIRIES

When fresh leads come to light on old cases, rarely is it possible to bring back the original investigators. They will almost certainly be working on other assignments. Previous to his phone call to Sergeant Porterdale, the gifted, clever Chief Inspector Reginald Morgan was instructed to familiarise himself with the York file. Information recently received claimed that a Lord Peter Fairfield of Oakwood had been on more than friendly terms with Constance York. This had not been known on the earlier investigation. The information had been given in a brief letter by a person who did not leave a name, the envelope addressed to *The Commissioner, Scotland Yard*.

Morgan opened the file and read it over twice. Margaret Williams came into the room.

'You look as if you've lost a pound and found a penny,' she remarked.

'It's this file. Not run-of-the-mill. Someone cool, calculating and highly intelligent. Someone who must have known she took capsules and had opportunity. Whoever planted the poison did it in such a way that the victim eventually would self-administer it. A delayed murder – ingenious. No need for an alibi because the murderer would be elsewhere when the death took place. So simple yet so clever. You know, Margaret, if ever we find who's

24

responsible, it will be almost impossible to prove in a court of law. All that was needed was to buy the product, substitute the poison for the granules of medicine, pop it in the bottle with the others, give it a shake and wipe the bottle clean of fingerprints. That poor woman, playing Russian roulette with herself. Not knowing one of them would painfully end her life. It makes me shudder to think of it.'

He referred to the file again. 'There were 11 capsules in the bottle when they found her dead. According to the file, these relief medicines are taken twice a day. One in the morning and one last thing at night. A bottle contains 30 when sold... what I would dearly love to know is how many were in the bottle when the alien capsule was added or replaced.'

'How would that help?' Margaret asked.

'I'll make a supposition that whoever did it hoped for the best odds of being well out of the way when it happened. Full bottle makes it 29 to 1 that she would take the fatal one the first time, 28 to 1 the next time and so on. It's hardly likely the bottle was full; the cap has a security seal that must be broken and torn off before use. No, at a guess, let's say somewhere in the region of two thirds full... that makes the odds 19 to 1 or, put another way, any time within nine to ten days. If my assumption is anywhere near correct, then the date would roughly be... let me see.' He thumbed through the pages again. 'Ah, she died on the fifth of August. That could mean the bottle was tampered with that number of days earlier. Sometime in the last quarter of July. All this is hypothetical, I know.'

'Hypothetical or not, it sounds good to me. You're beginning to sound like a detective. Anything else?' Her tone of voice sounded supportive.

'Fingerprints... one print not identified in the bedroom, does not prove positively that the owner of the print had anything to do with her demise. A one-off affair, perhaps. Ships that pass in the night.'

She grinned at that. 'Anything more?'

'Not a lot. I've no idea on how the poison was got hold of. Not that difficult to obtain, I have been advised in the past. I'm sure whoever was responsible didn't sign for it at a chemist's. Now for the information that brought me into the case. Is the information genuine or is someone wasting police time? Did this lord really know this York woman, and why the time lapse in letting us know?'

'Well, the best of luck on this one,' she said. 'I think you're going to need it.'

The day before his appointment with Lord Peter Fairfield, Morgan went along to the nearest chemist's and purchased the same brand of allergy capsules. On returning to his office, he tore off the seal and opened the bottle, emptying the contents onto the desk. He counted out 11 and put them back into the bottle. He then wiped his prints off with his handkerchief, carefully holding the bottle by its screw top cap. Using one of the police specimen bags and leaving the top unsealed, he put it in the inside pocket of his jacket.

CHAPTER SIX

FAIRFIELD MANOR

Morgan drove his car through the large gates. He presumed the estate had been in the Fairfield family for many years, and in those earlier years had employed many servants – as they were then called – for a mere pittance in wages. He imagined three full-time gardeners, horses about the place, stable lads, a butler and so on. Although there was no evidence, he got the impression that flower beds that once were had now been grassed over, cutting the work down to just a motor mower. He also visualised the transformation of its herbaceous borders converted to shrubberies, again in the interest of labour saving and the times we live in.

Chief Inspector Morgan was announced as plain Mr Morgan by the housekeeper when shown into the well-lit study.

Peter Fairfield sat at his desk. He looked up and smiled thinly. 'Mr Morgan, is it, Chief Inspector? Most considerate, most considerate. But it's of no consequence to anyone knowing a chief inspector is calling on me.'

'I'm obliged you were able to see me.'

Peter ushered him to take a seat. 'I've no idea of the reason why you are here, but I'm sure you will make it clear.' He ventured, 'It can't be anything to do with that unsettling one-off phone call I had; that was some time ago. Whoever it was must have realised that a practical joke of that nature would not be well received. Either that, or a wrong number was dialled and that's why no other calls were made.'

Morgan wasn't expecting that at all. Lord Peter would now be even more unsettled when he heard what Morgan had to say. 'You are quite right, I'm not here about any phone call. Now you've mentioned it, it could be relevant and related to why I have called on you. Tell me everything from the beginning, sir, every little detail if you please.'

'Don't waste both our time; it's so trivial.'

'Go on, please. I'll explain later.'

'If I must... now let me think... I was at my desk, here in this very room when the call came. It was on the twenty-second of July. I answered and heard – these may not be the exact words, but something like, "I have information that would be embarrassing to you if it were made public." I said "what information" and asked who was speaking, and the reply was "never you mind" or something like that. I said "go to hell" and replaced the receiver. Heard nothing since. What I can't understand is why you're so interested.'

'Was it a male or a female?'

'Can't be 100 per cent sure, deepish voice... female.'

'Do you believe it was an attempt at blackmail?'

'They'd be wasting their time.'

'Did you tell anyone about the call?'

'Only my son to begin with – I should have known better than telling him. Then it wasn't long before everyone else in the family knew, and one or two others no doubt. Some were convinced that I was keeping something back from them.'

'And were you?'

'Of course not! That's why I was so open about it to my son. Now what's all this leading up to?'

Morgan began calmly and slowly: 'We received an unsigned brief letter, the content not too dissimilar to your own phone call, implicating you in one of our former investigations. The accusation only saying that you were on more than friendly terms with this person.'

'That's incredible.' Peter's voice mellowed. 'What sort of investigation?'

'Unfortunately, murder.'

'Good gracious, whose, for God's sake, and why implicate me?'

Morgan answered with another question. 'Did you know and were you on friendly terms with a Constance York of Orange Tree Court, Croydon in Surrey?'

'Never heard of the woman,' Peter said sharply. 'You said "did" and "were"; is she the one that's been murdered? And the one whom I'm supposed to be involved with?'

'You are very astute, yes, she died on the fifth of August this year.'

'I was in Corfu then,' Peter said, uneasy but relieved.

'Purely for the record, what date was it when you left to go on holiday?'

'The second of August.'

'Why do you imagine you've been singled out in this way? Twice now someone making accusations of a sort. I don't understand the time gap between them. Have you made an enemy, say, over the last six months?'

'No one springs to mind. I have naturally in life and business upset one or two people, but they'd get their kicks at my expense by selling me duff shares. All my staff have been with me a number of years. No animosity in that quarter.'

'Just one other thing, you'll appreciate I have to ask.' Morgan carefully removed the bottle of capsules by its cap from his inside pocket. He said casually, 'Do you know of anyone who is in the habit of taking these?'

Peter took hold of the bottle. 'What are they?' He read the label. 'No, no one. A strange question... why do you ask me that?'

'If you don't know of anyone it's of no consequence. It may have helped if you did, that was all.'

Peter handed back the bottle unconcernedly, Morgan returning it carefully to his inside pocket.

'I don't like it. I don't like it at all. This leaves a nasty taste in the mouth,' Peter said. 'What the hell is going on?'

'I'm sure it does, sir; I'm sorry. I may have to see you again. I'll give you my card. Please get in touch with me if you have any more calls on any other matter whatsoever.'

'I certainly will. I want to know who this scandalmonger is, as much as you want to catch your murderer. You have my full support to openly get to the bottom of it.'

'It pleases me to hear you say that, sir; makes my job that much easier with no objections if I have to go on asking questions.' Morgan knew he was on thin ice taking notice of unsubstantiated accusations which ordinarily would be dismissed. As the accusations involved an unsolved brutal murder he just had to follow it through, even though there might be nothing to show for it. 'I'm obliged for your cooperation, sir; thank you.'

'You're welcome, but you leave me in a state of dismay and bewilderment.'

Leaving Lord Peter, Morgan was wondering whether he'd been told the truth. He drove for about an hour, then stopped his car at a roadside café and went inside. He was not hungry but wanted the toilet and fancied something to drink. He sat at a table and took out one of his two notebooks from his pocket. The black book was for official notes and official reports. The other, a red, was used for personal thoughts which he dared not trust his memory to retain. He drank his tea and ordered another. He wrote in the red book the following: *Did Fairfield know Constance York intimately? Was the third print in her bedroom his? Had he knowledge of her complaint and the opportunity to have planted the poison capsule before conveniently going on holiday abroad? What was the motive? Why did someone write to the Yard with Fairfield's name in connection with the dead York woman? Were both the call and note made by the same person and why?* He sighed and returned the notebook to his pocket.

Morgan had obtained fingerprints from Lord Fairfield in an unethical way. His unorthodox methods and devious mendacity had been partly responsible many times for success. This, he assumed, was why the commissioner's office turned a blind eye at times. He had got the prints on the bottle handed to Peter Fairfield at their meeting. And of course Fairfield had given them unwittingly when he had taken hold of the bottle.

The following day, comparisons were made at the Yard and found them not to match. Morgan was notably disappointed. He knew now that if he was to proceed, he might at some time have to contact members of the Fairfield family and employees. It would be problematic with so little to go on.

CHAPTER SEVEN

SURPRISE INVITATION

Morgan had a phone call. It was Pamela Fairfield. She told him her father had shown her his card; she was concerned and wanted to see him.

'I know this phone call is a bit unusual. I have been given two tickets for tomorrow's performance of a comedy play at the Globe. Is it at all possible, at such short notice, for you to be my escort? We could have a bite to eat after the play and talk. I hope I'm not being too forward in asking you to do this. If you refuse, I quite understand. We could meet up some other time.'

Morgan was very intrigued. He couldn't let this opportunity to talk to another Fairfield go by. 'I've never been asked out before by anyone. Most people are not that keen to speak to me, being a detective. I'd be more than happy to. The chat may even ease your concern,' he said encouragingly. 'Perhaps you could help me in some way or other.'

'Of course, if I'm able to.'

'That's good of you. Thank you.'

'We can meet in front of the theatre. Will seven o'clock be okay? I'll be wearing a light grey raincoat. Sounds like a movie, doesn't it?'

They met as agreed and shook hands. Her shoulder-length hair and make-up, moderately done, suited her face. She looked quite attractive.

Inside the lights dimmed and the curtains rose on the first act. When the interval came they went into the bar. Pamela seated herself at a table while Morgan went to order drinks. The bar was becoming crowded and she placed her coat on the empty chair opposite so that it could be seen to be occupied. Fingering a tablemat idly, she felt a hand on her shoulder. She looked up to find it belonged to Basil Broadwater.

'Hello, Basil. It's a small world.'

Basil's face showed no sign of geniality. 'I'm disappointed, Pam. I could have been with you tonight, not someone who looks more like hired help.' There was no hint in his voice to suggest he was joking. Not even a smile.

Pamela sensed he was seriously jealous. 'Hired help! He's dressed as smartly as you are. You're a snob, Basil. Would you tell him that to his face? I doubt it. In any case, it's nothing to do with you who I choose to go out with. I've never given you any indication that our relationship is anything other than colleagues, have I?'

Basil did not respond to the rejection.

Morgan paid for the drinks and pocketed the change. With one glass in each hand he edged his way gently through the crowd gathering around the bar.

Basil spotted him advancing towards them. Struggling to find some of his former charm by breaking into a smile, he said, 'Just my way of a pun; see you later.' He moved away hurriedly.

'You look a bit put out,' Morgan suggested, placing the drinks on the table.

'One of my muddleheaded workmates trying to be possessive,' she said. 'That's the last time I'll invite him down to Oakwood.' Feeling obliged, she gave a little more explanation. 'I work with Mary Austin, Joan Taylor and Basil Broadwater. I have invited all three on different occasions to spend some time at the manor. They've been company, and Dad seems to like me bringing someone down with me from time to time. I suppose if I'm honest, I like to show off a little of how fortunate we are to have a place like Fairfield Manor. I'm afraid Basil has got the idea that him being invited a few times means more to it than there actually is. I do believe he thinks of you as a rival, bumping into us here together.'

'I'm in the wrong league to be a rival. My income wouldn't keep you in the manner to which you are accustomed,' Morgan said with a big smile.

'I work for a living, the same as you. In any case, when I do look for a man to settle down with, money and position will not be the overriding factors,' she retorted defensively.

'I can't argue with that,' Morgan wryly said.

The bell rang, denoting the last call to theatregoers that the second half of the performance was about to begin. They drank up hastily and made their way back to their seats.

When the play ended and they were outside breathing the chilled air, they decided a hot meal in an Italian restaurant was not a bad idea. They had not far to walk, finding one just off the main street. As they settled themselves at a table for two, Morgan spoke: 'Now we can have that chat; what's on your mind?'

'It's Dad; he hasn't a clue what's going on. I can see it's getting him down. The nasty phone call, and now this letter to Scotland Yard, which has a more serious implication. He said he told you the truth but wasn't convinced you believed him.'

'I've no reason to doubt him whatsoever. He came across as genuine. It's not as though he's being accused of anything other than intimately knowing a lady that has been murdered. It's not the police that are making the accusation. He said he hadn't known her and I must accept that as the truth. I can't fully commit myself but, if it's any help, I believe him; you can tell him that.'

'Thank you, I will; that should take some weight off his mind. You said I may be able somehow to help you.' She looked at him enquiringly.

'The problem I have is to follow up on this unsolved brutal murder. The anonymous letter involving your father is difficult to handle. The only next move I have open to me is to compile a list. Would you be offended if I asked you to jot down all your family members?'

'I'd be only too pleased,' she said. Taking from her handbag a notebook, she tore out a page and promptly wrote down all the names and addresses of her relatives.

'Thank you very much, sorry, I have to have all the details. It's nothing personal. I will need to speak to someone - discreetly – who wouldn't mind giving me the names of all the people who work for and come in contact with your father. That's asking a lot, I know.'

'There's his private secretary. John French is not the type of man to blab about you meeting him or what you discuss.' She wrote down his role and where he could be contacted.

Morgan was quiet for a while, then he said, 'Let's change the subject. Did your father enjoy his holiday on Corfu? I know it's a while back now, but he mentioned it to me.'

'One thing he told me that made me laugh. He went to a taverna; he ordered fish. It came to him whole, head… tail… the lot; gutted, of course. The fish's head was enormous, with thick lips and bulging eyes starring pitifully at him from one side of the plate. He'd never seen a fish quite like it before. The only way he was going to eat any of it was if he covered its head over with a lettuce leaf. He never ordered fish again whilst he was there.' She looked across at him and smiled.

Morgan grinned back at her. 'I can understand his feeling; being looked at while you eat your victim, with its big eyes watching you in the act, is not for most Brits, who are so used to having their fish served up to them in fillets. Sorry, I'm making it sound like a crime scene.'

Their meals arrived and they ate heartily. After they had finished, and drunk coffee, they left the restaurant. Morgan said, 'Thank you for a very pleasant evening. I hope I haven't bored you with my company. Detectives are not noted for the best of conversations, only for asking questions.'

'Not at all; it's me who should be thanking you. I had a bit of a cheek asking you out. I'm pleased you accepted.' She paused. 'I hope I haven't got you into any trouble for seeing me socially. That I have not compromised you in any way in the job you are doing, and with your superiors.'

'At this stage in my investigation, you are not a suspect. Something, though, to reflect on. Your father gets that phone call before he goes away. He hears nothing more until I turn up with another accusation. I could be way off the mark, but doesn't that tend to show that whoever is doing it is someone who has a good knowledge of the Fairfield family? Someone close, perhaps... but why are they doing it? And how does it fit in place with an unsolved murder?'

CHAPTER EIGHT

WESTMINSTER OFFICE

Morgan wasted no time when the new week began. The offices of Lord Peter Fairfield were situated on the third floor in a block not far from Westminster Bridge. They were smaller than he had anticipated; nevertheless they were prosperous looking. The staff there consisted of John French, another man and two women. As he entered the outer office, the sound of a printer churning out information on continuous sheets met his ears. Having made his presence known, he had to wait for a while before he could be seen by John French.

When eventually they were alone in the private secretary's office, Morgan said, 'Sorry to disturb you at your place of work. Pamela Fairfield suggested you'd be the best one to have a word with.'

'Yes, she got in touch with me to put me in the picture,' French said.

'You know, then, why I'm here?'

'Yes; well, not entirely.'

'You know about the letter and the accusation.'

'Yes.'

'I had to make a start somewhere. It's a delicate situation. Anonymous phone calls – it would seem – are always made from public phone boxes. Those and unsigned letters are generally ignored for what they really are. When a murder or bomb threat is involved, they have to be taken seriously. I would be grateful, if you don't mind, for a list of names and addresses of all who work here, their status and how long they've been in Lord Fairfield's employment as part-time or full-time employees.'

French listened patiently without interrupting.

Morgan continued, 'I'm afraid I have to burden you further by asking for details of the staff at the manor, his business associates and anyone else that comes to mind who has or has had dealings with him.'

French gave him an exasperated look. 'That's one heck of a task. Pamela has a lot to answer for. Have you any idea of how many there are sitting in the House of Lords? No chance! You've cleared this with my employer—'

Morgan cut him short. 'He's fully supportive because of his unwelcome involvement. I'm aware that I may put a lot of people's backs up. A large percentage of my questions are irrelevant to the people I ask, but then I don't know that at the time of asking. I do not question purely for some kind of private curiosity. I'm just feeling my way. The sooner these are over and done with, the better for all concerned.'

'Yes, of course; I didn't mean to sound flippant. I'll do what I can. It could take a while if there are a lot of incoming calls.'

French went to another room and attended to the listing that Morgan had asked for. He returned and handed the list he'd made to Morgan, who was drinking a cup of coffee that had been brought to him. 'I've done my best," French said. "I'm sure it's not all you expected. There's nothing more I can add. Peter's friends and associates, I find difficult to give adequate information about. There are so many of them.'

'I didn't expect miracles. A few more points and I'll get out from under your feet; I'm sure you are a busy man.'

'Fire away, I'll do my best.'

'The other man that works here and the two women: how much contact do they have with their employer?'

'Hardly any; he sees them when he's here and passes the time of day with them, that's all.'

'Has anyone that you can think of showed resentment towards your employer?'

'No, no one, at least not in my presence.'

'He's not a saint,' Morgan said smilingly.

'No one is… I can't for the life of me believe anyone having hatred enough for a vendetta.'

'Is there anything, no matter how small or insignificant, that you can tell me? How about the spite of a woman? I'm informed Lord Fairfield is a widower.'

John French looked at him reproachfully. 'Nothing… really, you don't expect me to answer that, surely. It's not my business to know how he spends his time socially.'

'No, let's leave it at that. Give me a call on this number if anything comes to mind later.' He handed French his card.

John French was quiet for a while and then said, 'On the list I gave you, you'll find the name of Wally Spake. He drives for Lord Peter and takes care of the grounds and other small jobs around the place. Wally's a good sort, we get on well, calls a spade a spade, doesn't mince his words. You may or may not learn something helpful talking to him. When Wally left the navy on pension he joined his wife in Oakwood, because poor old Bill Ebson – the cook's husband – had passed on a short time before Wally was due to come out of the navy.'

'I'll let you get on. Thank you for your time and help.'

'You're most welcome,' French replied, pleased Morgan was leaving.

Not revealing who he was, Morgan spoke casually to the other members of staff on his way out, satisfying himself of what they all looked like, and making him very little the wiser.

CHAPTER NINE

SCOTLAND YARD

The day was bitterly cold. Morgan was thankful to get out of the chilly wind and inside. He found Margaret Williams adding papers to his 'in tray' as he walked in.

'Morning, Margaret.'

'Morning, Chief.'

Morgan wore no hat or gloves. He removed his coat and muffler and hung them on the stand in the corner of the room. He rubbed his hands together to bring back circulation. He then handed her a folded sheet of paper.

'Make a copy, please, and let me have it back, will you?' Morgan requested. 'Have the names checked out – I've little hope you'll come up with anything. Much piled up?' he asked dubiously.

'Afraid there is,' Margaret replied. She stood half smiling at him, waiting for his reaction to the paperwork in hand.

Morgan admired the way she looked in her dark blue skirt and white blouse. 'Make yourself comfortable,' he said, smiling back at her.

Margaret was fond of Morgan; his manner was always good-humoured towards her.

He sat down behind his desk and began to sort out from the pile the least important items, putting them to the bottom of the wire tray. Taking a memo from the top of his newly formed pile, Morgan said, 'Ah, fresh evidence in the Gifford case... good. Dig out the file and pass it back to Ferguson – put this memo with it. Should make his day, this. He's been a bit under the weather since the disappointment last time. Now, let's see, Ryan to join him as his scribe. May – with some work – lead to a conviction the second time around. Never say never, I'm—'

The phone interrupted. Margaret took the call. 'Yes, sir, he's here... no, I see, no need to disturb – I tell him... I – well – yes, of course.'

Morgan turned his attention from the papers and raised his eyebrows at her questioningly.

'Assistant commissioner wants to see you in an hour. Not before, he emphasised. Got somebody with him at the moment,' Margaret explained.

Morgan put his hand to his mouth and coughed to clear his throat. 'That is uncommonly benevolent of him,' he said dryly. Margaret grinned; some mutual understanding passed between them.

Morgan continued delegating some of the work in hand to her from the pile and reading aloud other items. When the subject of burglary turned up, Margaret's voice became less controlled; she spoke angrily. 'Why is it that some people glamorise the role of a burglar? I think a burglar is one of the lowest forms of scum on this earth. It broke my heart last Christmas,' she said heatedly, 'when I heard of a break-in at a house on Christmas Eve. They took all the children's Christmas presents from under the tree. How much lower can a human being get?'

'I couldn't agree more, Margaret,' Morgan said consolingly, 'and no comfort at all to the children when the police failed to retrieve their stolen presents. There's no satisfaction to any of us, if something was staring you in the face you never saw, or a question you should have asked was never asked, or a lead you should have followed up you missed. That can eat away at you at times. It's always there at the back of your mind, and you say to yourself, "Could I have done more? Is it my fault that they got away with it?"'

Because of his regular abruptness, Assistant Commissioner Michael Willoughby was not the easiest of men to get along with. He was, however, respected for his fairness and for standing up for subordinates if he felt the slightest need to do so.

Morgan knocked lightly on the door of his room exactly one hour after he had phoned. A voice from within called, 'Come!'

Willoughby greeted him in his usual brusque manner. 'Sit down,' he directed.

Morgan felt like a dog that was being put though his paces at Crufts.

An onlooker could be forgiven for believing that the two men's roles were the other way around at the Yard. Willoughby's suits of clothing all looked as if they were a size too large for him; today he wore dark brown. His large-rimmed spectacles lay on a squat nose. His hair was thinning and brushed across his scalp to cover bald patches.

'Just a word on the York affair – an update, if you like. I note in your report that this Lord – er – Fairfield denies knowing the woman. Also a twist we hadn't expected, ugh!, in the shape of a derogatory phone call received by himself. You go on to say that the unidentified print in Miss York's bedroom is not his. Did you ask him for his fingerprints?' Willoughby lowered his head and peered over the top of his glasses.

Morgan looked him straight in the eye. Bending the truth, he said, 'I asked Lord Fairfield to look at a bottle of Algi'rel, one identical to the one containing the deadly capsule that killed her. I asked him if he knew anyone that took them – I wanted to see the expression on his face, some reaction, anything, something, but his face remained that of a poker player. It was purely by chance that I remembered afterwards that his prints were on the bottle, so I had them compared.'

Willoughby took out a handkerchief and wiped his nose vigorously. 'I don't believe a damn word of it. You're too good a cop for just remembering.' He half smiled, the first sign of warmth toward Morgan since his entering the room. 'I take it for granted that after comparison his prints were destroyed.'

'Yes, sir, naturally, and no one knew whose prints they were comparing.'

Willoughby nodded. 'Good. Now tell me, where do you go from here? – if anywhere.'

'A good question, sir. As yet I've only familiarised myself with his office staff; that leaves his home staff, the rest of his relations and associates – business or otherwise. A lot of tact would be needed for that; I haven't strong enough grounds. In my favour is that I have Peter Fairfield's blessing to get to the bottom of who is causing all this trouble for him. There has to be a connection between the York murder, the phone call and the note. I've no idea what that connection is.'

'Having a deep belief is hardly enough,' Willoughby muttered, before adding emphatically, 'It would be unfortunate to come up with only a bogus timewaster.'

'If this character's got something concrete, why the hell doesn't he or she come forward in the proper manner? Let's concentrate for a moment on this person. What have we got? Someone of indeterminate age who may have made both communications. The first, we've only Lord P's word for it. The second we know is fact. Why was his name put forward? There's got to be a good reason. On my paperwork is a sister of Lord P's deceased wife; she lives in Kew. I might have a word with her,' Morgan said vaguely.

Willoughby looked over the top of his glasses again, then asked, 'Why her of all people?'

'Just someone to speak to who's well away from Oakwood. I have to be very careful of what I say and who I say it to. That's what you expect of me.'

'We're still no closer as to why this York woman was murdered,' Willoughby remarked.

'If Constance York was silenced for something she knew, perhaps threatened to use, she may have been given an undertaking; let's say payment by a certain date for what she had. That promise would have made her hold her tongue for a while. It would have given the one being threatened time to carry out a plan. Someone not the type to panic or be ruffled by it. The removal of Constance York need not be carried out speedily. Just make sure she died before the date she was expecting payment. This may explain why the killer could afford to wait, using an ingenious way of achieving it and being far away when it happened. Not knowing what sort of woman she was in life, it's hard to imagine whether she could be liked or hated. I might be doing Constance York a terrible injustice. She mightn't have been the blackmailing type of woman at all, but she had to die in someone's reckoning.'

'Hmm, all very baffling. Well, carry on as diplomatically as you can. One anonymous short letter, giving us a name of someone who is said to have been on more than friendly terms with this murdered woman, hardly gives us all the time in the world to spend on it, or free rein to go upsetting a lot of people because of it. Tread carefully. If you find yourself getting nowhere in the next week or so, then sadly the whole thing may have to be dropped,' Willoughby said, and he stood up from his seat, bluntly intimating the end of the meeting.

CHAPTER TEN

ANOTHER KILLING

It was a great surprise to Morgan when a sudden addition to the York case came to light. Nothing near what he had expected at all. Another anonymous phone call would have been more in keeping to what he had in mind. Someone stirring up a hornet's nest was hardly likely to have stopped where they apparently had, he felt sure. But this news was incalculable. What on earth was going on?

It had taken only a short time to reach a positive identification of a body found – almost, one could say in a macabre sort of way, with good fortune – when gale force winds brought down and uprooted trees in Slindon woods. Mother Nature had uncovered the corpse of Henry, brother of the ill-fated Constance York.

Workers assessing damage and clearing the debris of tangled timber reported their gruesome discovery in all haste to the local police, who on arrival at the scene cordoned off the area with the usual array of bright coloured ribbons on poles. The way in which Henry's life had been taken from him was far removed from the unhurried, planned death of his sister. He had been killed by a single blow to the back of the head from behind with a blunt instrument.

Detective Inspector Pringle of Sussex CID was in charge. He was a good young detective but tended to have little patience at times. Customary cooperation and exchange of information with Scotland Yard matched names and highlighted Morgan's involvement. As further details were related, little doubt was in the minds of both Morgan and Pringle that the two cases were connected.

'A rum business,' Pringle said, when the two eventually met. 'Brother and sister, eh... my, my. Stroke of luck, that storm. Trees went over, and up came roots. Brought him right out of the ground. Horrible shock to the one that found him. Shallow grave of course, buried just under the surface. Covered by old leaf mould and fresh autumn leaves. Scuffmarks and vegetation on heels gave signs of the body being dragged through part of the woods. Feasible assumption to say at night. Can't see anyone taking the chance during the day – can you? Driven down from... God knows where. Or the blow may have been struck in the woods.'

'Was he light enough for a woman to have dragged him?'

'Oh yes, he was only of small build. There again, there could have been two who took him there. One may have been lookout whilst the other took care of the dumping. We just don't know.'

'How long had he been dead?' Morgan asked eagerly.

Pringle referred to his notes and gave the experts' findings.

After a slight pause Morgan remarked, 'Not that long after the letter to the Yard... I wonder.'

'You think he may be your mysterious informer? Topped for what he knew?'

'You could put it like that.' Morgan grinned. 'It's one possibility. Records have it that after attending to his sister's affairs and funeral, he'd returned to his work abroad. The idea of him being back in this country hadn't entered my head. How exactly was he identified?'

Pringle looked pleased with himself. He put his finger to his ear and gave it a rub before replying. 'Without a lot of help, it might have taken a hell of a lot longer. The speed at which we get cooperation from Europe nowadays is incredible. The body had no identification. There was absolutely nothing in his pockets. I examined the label on the inside of his jacket and jotted down the tailor's name, found subsequently to be European. Another pointer being a small coin that had found its way through a tiny hole in the lining of his pocket. We believed we were dealing with a man visiting or returning from overseas. Well, after that – you know the drill. Missing persons, hotels, guesthouses, docks... flights to and from airports etcetera. The breakthrough came when we obtained a list of passengers from Air Continental. A list of people that had paid for return flights but hadn't turned up to take them in the time scale we were working on. You'd be surprised how many, not turning up for one reason or another. But they invariably ring the airport to cancel or make other arrangements. Hardly any don't turn up without a word, after paying a packet for return flights. Names were matched from flight arrivals. One name was given that had booked a return but never left the country. We were fortunate to interview the passenger who sat in the seat next to him, who said she had a good conversation with him. Told her he was staying at a flat in Bromley, rented through an estate agent also in Bromley.'

Morgan broke in, 'A stone's throw away from Croydon. Hmm.'

Pringle agreed and continued doggedly: 'He'd booked this flat from Bellman and Westcott. They gave us the address. Had to get them to open up, produce a search warrant before they'd do so. Apparently the owner goes away for a few months each year and makes a bit of money by leasing the flat for a month or more at a time. On searching the rented accommodation we found his passport. Checks and records proved the body in Slindon woods was him.'

Morgan's admiration for Pringle was high on how far he'd progressed in such a short time. 'Any indications of a struggle or that the murder took place in this flat?'

Pringle answered without hesitation. 'No, definitely not. No evidence to suggest that. The last occasion he was there, he'd spruced himself up prior to going out. He'd shaved but hadn't put his shaving gear away. Shaving brush and razor still lay on the sink. His discarded clothing lay untidily on the bed where he'd left it after changing. Seemed in a hurry to go out, leaving any tidying up until he returned – which of course the poor sod never did.'

'A pity nothing found as to whom he'd set out to meet. A woman, perhaps, he'd been so fussy on his personal appearance for,' Morgan said keenly.

'Might well have been,' Pringle uttered. 'That's one possibility, but who knows, he could have been fussy whoever he met.'

After some thought, Pringle said, 'There's still a lot more we can learn about this man, his background, of where he lived and worked, I'm thinking. Something to tie up both murders would be too much to ask, but we have to try. It strikes me that the person responsible for Henry York's death didn't know or wasn't interested in where he was staying. His keys are missing, but no evidence of anyone else giving the place the once-over. Just got rid of his keys along with the other items he had on him.'

'Two heads are better than one, but are two bodies better than one?' Morgan said in a lighter tone of voice.

'I can't for the life of me figure out why anyone wants to take a life. Surely there are other ways to resolve things. You've got husbands doing away with wives or vice-versa. Why can't they just get divorced and be done with it?'

'Motives, as you are aware, range from the understandable to the bizarre. Financial gain, jealousy, hate, revenge, who knows? The criminally insane feel they have a divine right to embark on a crusade to rid the world of prostitutes or some other group in society. Murders done on the spur of the moment and others premeditated. Some not condoned but, in the crime of passion, understandable. Others are for such trivial reasons that the mind cannot envisage it. Who can fathom the workings of the human brain? In this case, I have a vague view of motive. I'll not mention it. I wouldn't like to say anything that might influence your own line of thinking and perhaps put you off on the wrong track.'

'I've an open mind,' Pringle said.

'There's no reason to believe that the sister had large sums of cash. The settlement from her divorce was enough to set her up in comfortable accommodation. Her job did not bring in excessive amounts of money and she had only a modest amount in savings when she died. The brother, as far as we are aware, may have had more than his sister, but I speculate that no one will benefit financially from his death.'

'The cleaning lady at the sister's home was high on the list for special attention initially, wasn't she?' Pringle remarked. 'She appeared to be in the perfect position to add the poison capsule to the bottle – having the run of the place, so to speak.'

Morgan began writing in his red notebook. Something had come out of the blue into his mind, and he had to make a note before he lost it. His attention returned to what

Pringle had said. 'Rather too obvious, though. And there was no sense made in her doing it. She lost money by the death of her employer, not gained. She was out of a part-time job. Constance York's ex-husband also gained nothing. He had amicably parted from her some two and a half years previously.'

'You haven't let the dust settle, by the sound of it.'

'Most of that is from the previous investigation,' Morgan replied, not wanting to take any credit for the work of others.

'There's so many motives to consider,' Pringle reflected.

'Anger, betrayal, blackmail, fear,' said Morgan meditatively.

'Yes, fear of being found out,' contributed Pringle.

'Gain, heat of the moment. Take your pick: retribution, vengeance, provocation, pleasure, reward, robbery with violence, witchcraft, ritual killings.'

'Are you trying to confuse me? Most of those wouldn't fit this case at all,' said Pringle irritably.

'I'm making too much of the options. But who knows what people will do in any given set of circumstances?' Morgan wondered why Pringle was so touchy. 'At the moment there's no clear picture.' He opened his notebook again. 'It's plain what I must do next. Someone found it necessary to get rid of both members of the York family. Being conventional, the answer should be found in their background somewhere – but where to start and how far back? Before you found the brother, I was almost in limbo but contemplating seeing people on this list with an awful lot of discretion.' He passed over the list containing 20 names or so. Pringle looked at the names keenly for a while, then handed the paper back.

'That's always the problem: the more people you see, the more the list grows. Running around and seeing all these individuals can be a mammoth task. What are your intentions?'

'I was thinking of shelving that list for a time, while the brother's side of the investigation is going on. See what you can turn up. On the other hand, perhaps not. I may go over old ground.'

'If you go back over ground already well trodden, those questioned won't be so happy the second time around.'

'I'll have to make doubly sure not to ask the same questions – come up with a few new ones.'

'Will the Yard eventually take over from here?' Pringle asked impatiently.

'That's not quite the case. You have to put up with the body of Henry York being found on your patch. Or, more appropriately, in your neck of the woods.'

'I like that,' laughed Pringle lightly.

'You carry on with the good work of Henry York. We obviously keep in touch with one another; a joint venture, if I can put it that way. Ah, well, on with exhaustive inquiries. You've done extremely well up until now. I wish you and your team success with what you have to do next. If you come across a photograph of both brother and sister together, I'd like a copy.'

Pringle tightened his lips and nodded. 'Yes, I'll make a note.'

Morgan cleared his throat. 'If you've no objection, I'll take a look around the flat in Bromley.'

'It's been left for that purpose. The estate agents are pressing for its release. I don't think there's any more to be gained from the place, but you're more than welcome,' Pringle stated a little coolly. 'We can make our way there now, if you like.'

The flat in question was on pavement level, being one of four in the large building: one self-contained flat to each floor. The other permanent tenants hardly noticed the comings and goings of one another, let alone the bottom flat. Likewise, neighbouring houses and others in the street kept themselves to themselves and had not seen a thing that could be classed as helpful to the police.

When they were inside, Morgan said reflectively, 'I won't keep you long; a quick look, then I'll be making a move.'

The two went from room to room diligently. As they did so, Pringle repeated some of the points already explained. Nothing had been altered and Morgan was able to see for himself exactly what Pringle had come across earlier. Morgan took particular notice of two second-hand paperback books that lay on the bedside table. He gave Pringle a probing glance. 'Just a small point.'

'What might that be?'

'These paperbacks: have you flicked through the pages?'

Pringle was slightly caught off guard. 'I – er... as a matter of fact, I do believe I did thumb through, hoping something useful might be amongst the pages. Nothing fell out. No five pound notes or anything else marked a page place,' he said glibly.

'What about anything scribbled? It's not unusual to find oddments written down on the inside of second-hand book covers.'

'One book is clean, in the other there are snippets, ad-hoc jottings – here, see!' Pringle showed notes made by some of the book's past assorted readers. 'If any of this scribble was made by the deceased, I can't see anything here that's liable to help us.'

'I dare say not, but you know as well as I do that sometimes the insignificant can be the downfall of the overconfident criminal. A secret is no longer a secret if any of it is written down. On the back page – the last entry – an 11-figure number. Might well be a telephone number. Do no harm to check it out,' Morgan said flatly.

Pringle wasn't amused; he raised his eyebrows and wrote the number down reluctantly. What sort of a time-wasting observation was that? he thought.

CHAPTER ELEVEN

RETRACING STEPS

In light of the brother's body being found, the Scotland Yard detective felt he had more than enough to continue with the original investigation.

Morgan rang the door bell at the home of the ex-cleaning lady to the late Constance York. She responded to find Chief Inspector Morgan standing there, smiling pleasantly. 'Mrs Ingles?' he inquired.

'Yes, the very same,' she said, a little restrained, and raising her eyebrows in an expression of *who the hell wants to know?*

Morgan showed identification. 'I'm sorry to disturb you, Mrs Ingles; my call, I'm afraid, is once again in connection with the cleaning post you had at Orange Tree Court.'

Her face showed slight trepidation. 'I suppose you'd better come in; I don't much like talking on doorsteps.'

Morgan followed her in and accepted a chair offered. 'I really must apologise for having to bother you yet again after all the anxiety caused previously,' he began gently. 'I do hope your life has not been affected too much by this tragic and depressing situation.'

She frowned. 'I had the feeling it wasn't the end of the matter. When I read about her brother in the paper – it sent a shiver down my spine, I don't mind telling you... in fact, I felt quite frightened. Don't forget I worked there. First her, now him – what have they got against them, that's what I'd like to know.'

'Yes, it's dreadful, must have been quite a shock... I'm sorry. I hope you will not find it too upsetting to talk about one or two things,' he said kindly.

'No, but it won't be easy. What exactly is it you want me to tell you? I've already said all I knew to the other policemen last time.'

'I'm most grateful – but, you see, my purpose in calling on you is more in the way of gaining knowledge of the sort of person Constance York was. I'd like you to fill me in on certain points of the woman herself. It's better hearing first-hand rather than reading what others have written.'

Mrs Ingles closed her eyes for a moment. 'It was me that gave the alarm that something was wrong the morning she was found dead. Oh, it was awful. I went regular, you see, three times a week. Monday and Wednesday mornings and Friday afternoons. I'd a key she'd given me. Mornings she'd gone before I'd arrived – as I told the others – so I had to have a key. That particular Wednesday morning I couldn't get in, so I knew she was still in there. I turned the key but the door was bolted. I thought she must be ill. I didn't know what to do at first and told the caretaker. He shouted and banged but it made no difference, so he phoned the police. When they came, they had to break in. They wouldn't let me in. A nice young policewoman said she looked terrible. Her face was all contorted and she was all curled up as if in agony – with her hands clasping her stomach—'

Morgan stopped the flow of what appeared to be painful memories. 'Please, I'm not endeavouring to make you go over what must be distressing all over again.'

'No... oh – thank you.'

'I take it you're not working at Orange Tree Court any more?'

'No fear of that, not me!'

Morgan casually gave her an appraising glance. He had not actually taken in what she really looked like in detail. She was quite an attractive woman, in her early forties. Perhaps slightly underweight for her height. She had blonde curly hair, cut short.

'How did you come to work for Constance York?' Morgan asked.

'It was because of the one I cleaned for before her. She recommended me. Connie didn't know her; she gave me a very good reference.'

'That was thoughtful of her.'

'Yes, it was – see, I never let people down. Always do my best. Not only cleaning, other things as well, like washing up, making beds and shopping and—'

'Quite commendable... When you worked for Constance York, was she an easy person to get along with?'

'Most of the time she was – although she could be bossy if she'd a mind to. Can't say she treated me badly. Never any disagreements. Always paid me regular, every Friday. If she weren't there, she left the money on the table.'

'Did you ever meet her brother? Henry.'

'Only the once – when he paid me off.'

'What did you make of him?'

'Well, I didn't see him for long. Didn't seem too upset at the time – very sympathetic and businesslike, he was.'

'Did you go to her funeral?'

'No; perhaps I should have done. I've thought about that a lot.'

'Did she receive much in the way of mail? Postcards especially may come to mind. In particular, anything other than post from her brother.'

'I can't help you there. I wasn't there every day, as I said.'

'How often would you speculate she and her brother corresponded?'

'Not a lot, as far as I know. Birthdays and at Christmas time – the odd letter on occasions. I wouldn't have known but for the foreign stamp. No, there weren't a lot of post I saw.'

'Did she ever speak of her ex-husband? Or anything about her marriage?'

Mrs Ingles looked thoughtful, cupping one hand under her chin. 'I got the impression there was no regret – I may be wrong. She never brought the subject up, other than when she explained she'd parted from her husband when I first started to work for her. As I say, she didn't seem too concerned.' Mrs Ingles slipped into deep thought for a moment. 'A woman knows things when she cleans for another. Ever since I've worked for her, there's never been any signs of a man's company left in the flat – that's not to say she didn't ever go out with any; I wouldn't know about that. And yet, I mean to say, they said someone had been in her bedroom other than me. I couldn't believe it.'

'What was her relationship with others in the block of flats? Didn't she ever ask at least one of them in for a cup of tea and a chat? Quite a natural thing to do once in a while.'

'From what I gather, she only passed the time of day with 'em – you know the kind of thing: commenting on the state of the weather or the odd smile when she passed one of 'em going out or coming in. As far as it is possible for me to say, she never made a friend of any of 'em. I never found any extra cups or glasses to wash up. Having said that, she always wanted to know of any titbits that I'd heard about the others resident there.'

Morgan smiled. 'Did she ever speak of her interests, hobbies, or anything she'd done after work or at weekends?'

'She bought magazines. She remarked once that she'd been invited to a wine party – no, a wine club or circle, that's what it was. I know she liked a glass of wine. There was always a couple of bottles in her kitchen.'

'Do you recall the name of this club or where it is? Or who gave her the invitation?'

'No, I don't recollect her saying.'

'I'd like you to concentrate very hard before you answer: was there, on any of the days you arrived at the flat, anything that you'd call out of the ordinary?'

There was a long pause. 'Ah, now, funny you should say that. Since you mentioned it, there was the once. I thought it unusual. You see, one morning when I came, the bed was made. I wondered why she'd made it herself. I always did it for her on the days I came. It was the same with the breakfast things; she'd washed them up and put them away. I mean, she never had a lot of time in the mornings. I remember having the feeling that I must be in her bad books for some reason, for her to have done that. I never did ask her why. I'd have felt awkward.'

'You didn't mention this to the other detectives!'

'No, they didn't ask me that sort of thing,' Mrs Ingles said curtly. 'It's only just come to mind since you've asked.'

It was Morgan's turn to ponder for a while. 'It could have been that she didn't sleep in her bed, and had therefore not breakfasted at the flat. She had in fact stayed out overnight.'

'Come to think of it, you may well be right. Never thought of that.'

'I don't suppose you'd remember when that was?'

Mrs Ingles closed her eyes and tightened her lips. She was silent for a good few minutes. 'Yes,' she exclaimed triumphantly. 'I remember it was towards the end of July... first of August. I'm sure now I tore off the page of the thirty-first from the calendar. Does that help? Is it important?'

'You may well have given another way of how someone could have had the opportunity of access to her medication; that's on the assumption that she stayed out overnight and took it with her. The question's been centred on how anyone got into her flat to do it. It's been assumed that the bottle was always kept in the medicine chest.'

Mrs Ingles face took on a serious and somewhat angry expression. 'Crikey! And to think what the other detective put me through over that. He damned well almost accused me! And the questions: did I have a lover in the flat? Blasted cheek. Anyone in from the phone company? Did I let anyone in the flat at any time? Where did I keep the key when I wasn't working there? Did my husband have access to it? I told him it was always kept in my handbag, no one else touched it, and my husband never rummages through my belongings.'

Graeme Biley, Constance York's ex-husband, was on edge when Morgan called on him. The restlessness – or was it resentment at being disturbed? – was plain by his manner. 'Haven't you people—' He cut himself short.

Morgan looked at him tolerantly. As was often required in his job, he endeavoured for a moment to find the most effective words to combat indifference. 'Have you no desire to help bring to justice the person responsible for the death of your ex-wife and now her brother?' he asked bluntly.

'That's not fair, that goes without saying... of course I do – but – well – it's just I thought that I wouldn't be implicated enough to be questioned again, and – after all this time – I'd be left alone as I have nothing at all to do with any of it.'

Morgan's tone became conciliatory. 'This won't take long, I assure you. Your help on a couple of points: that's the only reason I'm here. I'm attempting to find out why someone had reason to do away with both your ex-wife and her brother.' Morgan paused, then remarked, 'You surely must have asked yourself the same question: why on earth has someone done such terrible things?'

Graeme Biley shifted uneasily. 'I was devastated and horror-stricken when I heard, naturally... look here, I wasn't married to her for all that time without some affection towards her. She wasn't perfect – no one is. Occasionally she'd stick her nose in other people's business. We disagreed over that. I've often wondered what sort of lifestyle she had after we broke up, and why it ended up the way did. What she got up to, who she mixed with, I haven't the foggiest. I'm not uncooperative. I've a new life, remarried and quite happy.'

'You never kept in touch with one another after you parted?'

'No, we didn't. I moved here; that's how it worked out. She went her way and I went mine.'

'I understand you refused to give any details as to why your marriage failed. It's on record that you felt it was your own business and no one else's.'

Biley nodded. 'And so it is. The reason we parted is private and personal, has nothing to do with anyone, and is of no use to the police. What a ridiculous thing for them to be interested in.'

Morgan shook his head doubtfully. 'That depends. It would have been quite relevant if she'd left you for another man, for instance. That man could have been a separate line of inquiry into her death.'

'It was nothing like that – nothing of the sort. All I'll say is, we parted on agreeable terms without the need for solicitors.'

Morgan persisted impassively: 'You find you have difficulty in blaming the breakdown on yourself, on her, or both? Others are quite open on such matters.'

Biley said in an aloof tone of voice, 'I don't find it at all difficult.' Then he added in stronger tones, 'It's just none of any outsider's concern.'

Morgan changed tactics. 'How did you come to meet Miss York, as she was then?'

Biley calmed. 'I sat next to her in a theatre. We struck up a conversation and it went from there.'

'She went often to the theatre?'

'No, she was given a ticket by her brother. Apparently she wasn't that fussed on going, but he persuaded her to accept it as he'd paid and couldn't go that evening.'

'Where did she work at that time?'

'The same place she's always worked, in Bell Street.'

'Ah, yes, I have that address. Apart from her work, what other interests had she? I'm trying to establish and piece together anything that might be of use.'

'Very little, really... does one really, fully know another? Even when you live together? She didn't knit, certainly not baby clothes... or crochet. She wasn't interested in sport of any kind. She was an excellent cook, I'll say that for her. She smoked but very moderately. Reading, yes, a lot of that, and an interest in wine. She liked to try as many different kinds as she could afford. Some were rather expensive – I remember how she cursed if she'd paid a high price for a wine and then didn't like it.'

Morgan thought, why mention baby clothes? 'You had no children by your first wife,' he stated purposely.

'That was one of our differences,' Biley let slip.

'You wanted a family and she didn't?'

'Yes, exactly – you're a devious devil.'

Morgan was not offended. He was a devious devil. 'Wasn't the subject of a family discussed by both of you before you got married? She must have had her reasons for not wanting motherhood.'

There was something simmering in Biley's brain and it boiled over. 'I won't speak of her unkindly, but she went back on her word. In a nutshell, she was self first in this case. My views did not seem to matter, only her own. The abortion nearly—' He stopped short.

'Your wife had an abortion?'

'Oh, hell! You're not likely to leave me alone until I tell you. She became pregnant – my baby – and she had it terminated without a word to me. No consultation, just went ahead and did it. There, now you know. That was the final straw – from then on our relationship was never the same and never could be.'

Morgan said feelingly, 'I'm sorry, very sorry; I'll not mention it again. Just one last thing, then I'll get out from under your feet. How would you describe her brother? I mean, his behaviour in general. What sort of a man was he, how did you get along with him, and did he and his sister hit it off?'

'I'd say he was entirely the opposite to his sister... they seemed to hit it off quite well, to use your expression. Happy-go-lucky sort. Found him rather a pleasant fellow; didn't see him at all after he went abroad for his firm.'

'And the firm was?'

'I don't know the name. He was an illustrator of some sort.'

Morgan left him; he seemed genuine, although the best actors were not all on the stage. A thought sprang to mind that he had squeezed out a motive for murder: the one of hate. But why should it fester now, after two and a half years? And Biley had earlier been eliminated of suspicion. That was not to say one did not get others to do their dirty work, but no, the brother was also dead, it did not fit at all. There was the unexpected disclosure of the abortion. He put that out of his mind; what purpose would it serve? Biley had commented on his wife being meddlesome, but compared to Morgan's own prying she came across as Mother Superior, he mused.

The last call but one on Morgan's re-interview list was at Orange Tree Court. He found it seldom profitable to go over the same ground as his former colleagues, but he had the advantage of seeing their recorded interviews, so he could avoid repetition and try other avenues: an advantage his predecessors could not possibly have had. They were the pioneers and he acknowledged that fact.

To his surprise, he met no resistance to his questioning. In fact, the residents were only too pleased to be helpful. The exercise only confirmed what he had already been aware of – with one exception. If any of the occupants in the flats had wanted to entertain someone without being seen with them, they could have gone to the trouble at an appropriate time of opening the fire-door in the basement. The basement fire-door led to a small courtyard at the back of the block of flats where dustbins were kept. But why should anyone want to do that?

The last call found him in the offices in Bell Street where Constance York had worked. The small staff of a coach holiday booking firm consisted of a branch manager and two female assistants. The younger of the two women had filled the vacancy left by the late Constance York and was of no use to Morgan. The branch manager received him courteously. He was a heavyset man with a slight stoop, from many years of bending over a desk presumably.

'You were helpful the last time the police called, so I've read,' Morgan said.

'Well, what little I was able to say, I wouldn't have thought so. And, in any case, the police rarely tell you "have" or "haven't".'

Morgan could not restrain a slight grin. 'You must have done your best; that's all that's asked. Thank you.'

'Under the circumstances, it would have been insensitive of me to have done otherwise,' the manager said lightly.

'Sorry to go again over some things regarding Mrs Biley or Miss York, whichever you prefer. She worked here for a good number of years. Did she prove to be a valued employee?'

'Oh yes, quite reliable.'

'Did she have a weak or strong personality, would you say?'

'Forceful in her views.'

'Can you recall her ever having received private phone calls at work?'

'Not that I'm aware of. She may have had... wait a moment, I do remember once; she apologised. Said she wasn't expecting any. We don't encourage it. In an emergency it is quite acceptable, of course.'

'Could you tell me when?'

'Not exactly, but it wasn't that long before her death.'

'Did she ever show signs of dissatisfaction in her work?'

'On the contrary, as she commented more than once, she was quite satisfied with the many years she'd worked here.'

'You got on well with her?'

'Oh yes; you don't even have to like a person to get on with them. As long as they do what is expected and are amiable, then all goes smoothly.'

'Did you dislike her for any reason?'

'No, whatever gave you that idea? We got along quite well. I'm moved more than it shows. Even now, I still can't forget her smile. Just an ordinary working woman. Why such a terrible thing happened to her and now her brother is beyond me.'

'Have you any idea where she went at lunch breaks?'

'She lived far enough away not to go home. Brought sandwiches, ate them here. Some days she did shopping, I believe, and had a snack out somewhere sometimes.'

'Did she confide in you with her personal affairs? Talk about anything that was troubling her?'

'Dear me, no, never. Connie was a very private person. She may well have done so, of course, with her opposite female number in the office. A more natural thing to do, don't you think?'

Her opposite number was a motherly type, the type of woman one might well confide in. She was ushered in to Morgan by the branch manager, who was only too glad to speedily retreat to the outer office. Morgan continued in the same vein of questioning. His aim was to learn as much about Constance York's individuality and out-of-work activity as could be gathered. Bearing in mind what the cleaning lady had told him, he asked, 'Did she ever mention anything about her passion for wine?'

'I do remember once Connie saying that she'd bumped into a stranger at a wine store where they were both browsing the wines. This woman told Connie that she knew of a wine circle. The wine circle met several times a year. The members enjoyed the privilege of purchasing wines at

67

reduced prices. They also had a guest speaker at their meetings. This woman gave Connie the address and asked if she would like to go along one evening. She never did tell me where it was, or whether she went or not,' her old co-worker said.

CHAPTER TWELVE

LINK – PRINGLE REPORTS

Inspector Pringle was completing his progress report into the death of Henry York. He shrugged his shoulders. Morgan would be updated in due course. 'You always want more,' he reflected and muttered. On the other hand, he had something of the greatest importance. To be perfectly honest with himself, he was busting to see the reaction on the face of the Scotland Yard detective.

From when he had first been called in on the case, his attention had focussed on the lay-by not far from where the body had been found. The aspects of the coverage went again jerkily through his mind: no hope of tyre tracks. Not able to take plaster casts of tyre impressions; time lapse too great. Countless vehicles would have pulled off the road at that spot. Nevertheless, as a matter of routine soil samples were taken from the lay-by and from where the body was found. The weapon still not recovered, nor any of the personal effects of Henry York.

Cooperation had been commendable. Henry York had worked for a company with the name of Brinkly Technical Illustrations. Contract work for numerous firms. Some government work – nothing secretive – nothing on weaponry. Frankly, Pringle saw no logical argument to connect Henry York's death with anything to do with his employment.

One question that needed answering was why he had made the trip back to England in the first place. Staying put where he was would almost certainly have meant that he'd have been alive today. Gone over in Pringle's mind were three possibilities of why Henry made the journey. The first was company business, but that wasn't the case. Had he been summoned? Or had he come of his own accord? According to his employer, it had been the last one, to clear up urgent family business. What was that family business? As far as Pringle understood, Henry had settled all that not long after the death of his sister. There were no other family members living.

Pringle covered diligently all the normal investigative points before arriving at the all-important part of his summary: linkage. A list of names and places had been found in Henry's effects, removed from his office desk by the manager and kept in a neat bundle. These personal items were handed over to the police. The last name on that list was *P Fairfield, Oakwood, England.*

'There's your link, for what it's worth,' Pringle told Morgan, when they met.

'That is absolutely bloody marvellous – well done!' Morgan exclaimed with enthusiasm. 'I can hardly believe the good fortune, finding the Fairfield name written down in the possession of one of the Yorks – now, what can we make of that? And who are the other three on that list? And where do they fit in?' Morgan read aloud: 'J Dugdale, Medhurst. A Sloan, Lowplain. W Maxwell, Denchurch. Any ideas?'

'They mean nothing to me, apart from Medhurst, Lowplain and Denchurch being very small villages.'

'There's another slight quandary. Apart from "P" meaning Lord Peter, it could mean "P" for Phillip, the son, or, come to that, "P" for Pamela, the daughter even. So be it; makes my next move far easier, where perhaps it might have been awkward before. We must fully check on whether there is more than one P Fairfield living or who lived in Oakwood.' Morgan continued with the same thoughts running through his mind. 'Did the York woman stumble on something? If that was so, whatever she saw, heard or found out by chance must have been quite something. Enough for someone to make sure she never revealed it. Continuation along these lines of speculation: surmise Constance York was the one who made the telephone call to Lord Peter Fairfield. He tells her to go to hell. After a while Lord P tells his son Phillip, who in turn tells others. Without going over all the details again, whoever feels threatened sets about to remove the threat and succeeds. All is well; the brother Henry is naturally terribly shaken by what has happened to his sister but completely ignorant of anything known by her that got her killed. He comes over to sort out her belongings and to give her a decent funeral. Later, when he goes through her small personal possessions, he comes across – amongst other items – these names written in his sister's handwriting. He's curious. Our people went through all her belongings before they were handed over to him, but would hardly have gone to the extreme of taking notice of something so seemingly minor. He perhaps makes phone calls and learns the P Fairfield in Oakwood is Lord Peter Fairfield and is in parliament.'

'Why didn't he immediately pass any information over to the police?' said Pringle despondently.

'He must surely have known how dangerous it could be to go delving into things alone. But he didn't tell the police. Perhaps he felt it wouldn't be enough. Instead he comes again back to England. He can't find out anything about the other names on that list, so he writes to Scotland Yard and gives the name of the only one he knows to be checkable, hoping to restart our investigation. Henry may have had every intention of going to the police once he had enough to go on. By pursuing this slim lead on his own, all of a sudden he makes the guilty party vulnerable once more. I don't know how, but Henry keeps an appointment and is removed. The one who disposed of Henry's body in the woods was aware of him poking his nose into things that would be perilous.'

'It's a good scenario,' Pringle said, guardedly. 'Am I right in thinking that you are dispelling any guilt on the part of Lord Peter Fairfield, because of him telling the York woman to go to hell when she supposedly phoned him? Equally, Phillip Fairfield is in the clear because of his openness in telling others of the call. That leaves one only with the initial "P": Pamela... I can't believe it to be that easy.'

'No, neither can I... I have a strong conviction that Henry York made some notes on what he was up to, and kept them on him. As the keys in his possession were never recovered, and his pockets empty, they were destroyed. Can you go any further with your investigation into Henry's death? Is there any more you have to do?'

'Doubtful, I think we've gone as far as we can... any progress on your part?'

Morgan gave a strained smile and went on to give an account of all of his retraced steps.

'A strange case.' Pringle paused. 'Will we ever get to the bottom of it? Even though we have this extra ammunition?'

'I've had a thought. When I eventually get to the point of calling on the Fairfield clan, I don't intend to mention all the names on that list you came across. Only the first two – and our trump card, P Fairfield of Oakwood.'

'What have you in mind?'

'I don't know exactly, but it might be wise to keep something back.'

'Why don't we go straight away and tackle the three Ps and get to the truth?' Pringle put forward impatiently.

'I prefer to go all the way around the outside and gather all I can before going to the centre. The more we have, the more to tackle them with.'

Pringle said sheepishly, 'I hate to admit this, but since you've mentioned a wine club or wine circle... I dialled that number, you know, the one scribbled down in that second-hand book—'

'And?'

'Of all things, it was a wine store. I didn't ask the name or where it was – I'm sorry. I didn't think it relevant when I found out; it was so insignificant that I brushed it aside without a second thought. It still might not be relevant.'

'We didn't know the importance of the wine connection at that time, and obviously you didn't ask if the names of Henry or Constance York were familiar to them.'

'I did not. I just said "sorry, wrong number".'

'Not to worry; I quite understand it means nothing on its own. Slowly but surely things are beginning to fall into place. If this wine store has any relevance, we may be getting somewhere. Look, I'll tell you what we'll do. Let's go and have a drink at the Swan Tavern. I'll ring Margaret, get her to feed those names and places through the system. She can ring us back. While she's doing that, you can ring that number again and find out the name and whereabouts of this wine store. Don't ask any other questions; we'll give them a visit in good time.'

The two sat silently at a table in the Swan Tavern. Their drinks stood hardly touched in front of them. Pringle was impatient and had made his telephone call first, to the wine store. Then Morgan had made his.

Margaret returned the call just under an hour later. 'I'm sorry to have taken so long,' she said apologetically. 'I've cross- and triple-checked but I'm afraid there's nothing on file on any of them.'

Morgan thanked her for her effort, turned to Pringle and shook his head. 'No luck there, but never mind. Perhaps—' He stopped, then went on. 'Three little villages have three little churchyards. I've a hunch. Let's go down to the first village on that list. Where is it?'

Pringle unfolded the paper and looked. 'Medhurst. And the name is J Dugdale. You intend looking around churchyards? What purpose would that serve?'

'There's no better place to hide a body than a cemetery.'

'We're not looking for more bodies – are we? I don't follow.'

'No, I hope not. Two's quite enough, thank you. My brain plays funny tricks at times. It's just the mind dwelt morbidly on freshly dug graves. Don't ask me why I should dwell on that. I think detective work makes you think that way after a few years in the job. The soil is soft and unsettled. A cemetery in the heart of a big city is a risky place to go digging about at night. Whereas a quiet village churchyard is ideal. Think of it: all that has to be done is to dig down a few feet on a recent burial, dispose of another body – or anything else, come to that – then cover up again. Nobody would be expected to disturb the earth again to any great depth. In time they are grassed over and headstones are placed, but no more digging to be done.'

Pringle looked at Morgan and laughed. 'Excuse my insubordination: you're a comforting bugger to be with, I must say.'

Morgan grinned. 'Let's call it a day; I want to make an early start in the morning. Get yourself a good night's sleep.'

CHAPTER THIRTEEN

MEDHURST

Early the next morning, Morgan and Pringle arrived in the beautiful secluded village of Medhurst. They saw immediately the little church spire through the trees and went directly towards it. The stone walls surrounding the churchyard were low, and Pringle thought of what Morgan had said the day before.

They walked briskly, for the air was cold. Following the low stone walls, they came upon the front entrance. Yew trees grew either side. Morgan opened a rickety swing gate – which had seen better days – and they passed through and under a heavy timbered archway to reach the grounds. There was little breeze. The place was as tranquil as one would expect. The quietness and peacefulness of their surroundings gave them both a feeling of humility as they trod the gravel path that led to the church itself.

'What have you in mind?' Pringle asked indulgently.

'Parish register in the main. As we're early, you start this side. I'll take the other, take a look at names on the gravestones. See if you can find any Dugdales.'

'Not quite my cup of tea, prowling around churchyards, I'd sooner be looking at the inside of the church,' Pringle fretfully responded.

They separated and began stooping over the stones, reading the inscriptions. Once they were off the gravel path and on the short clipped grass, conditions became rather damp underfoot. It could be seen the grounds were well kept and attended to regularly. Morgan smiled cynically at one epitaph:

> *You find me here beyond forlorn*
> *I did no asking to be born*
> *As true as sunshine lights the sky*
> *I didn't ask for me to die*
> *On these two things we have no voice*
> *You must accept there is no choice*

'How very true,' he acknowledged, and moved on.

He got so engrossed, he lost all sense of time and completely forgot about his companion. When he did raise his head, he found himself in part of the grounds that lay behind the church, where gravestones were of more recent dating. He came abruptly on one that made him startle: a stone inscribed *John Dugdale*. He stretched and rubbed the pit of his back that was beginning to ache, then hastily went in search of Pringle. He found him at length peering at a headstone dated 1889.

'We're not going back that far!' Morgan said with joviality.

Pringle straightened from his bent position and stood upright. 'My shoes are wet through,' he grumbled.

'Never mind that. Come with me.'

Morgan led the way to the grave of John Dugdale. 'What do you think of that?'

'I'm impressed,' Pringle said truthfully. 'He's dead, then.'

'Obvious, being where he is,' Morgan could not resist the temptation to say. 'No, I know what you mean,' he added quickly.

Polite coughing came to their ears from the direction of the rear door of the church. They both looked in unison. An elderly clergyman was walking slowly towards them. His raised eyebrows and quizzical expression signalled his surprise at their being there so early in the morning. 'May I be of some service, gentlemen?'

'Good morning, Vicar – er – not a very pleasant day,' Pringle said conversationally

'We must be thankful for what the Lord has provided,' the vicar retorted piously.

'Indeed, indeed we must," Morgan said. "Sorry to take it upon ourselves to be wandering around so early. Please do not be alarmed; we are policemen. My name is Morgan and this is my colleague Pringle.'

Pringle felt it rather a nice gesture of Morgan's not giving ranks. He very much appreciated being called Morgan's colleague.

The vicar looked perplexed. 'Oh, dear love of God, I do hope nothing dreadful brings you here. It's such a close community. What has happened?'

The two policemen glanced at each other searchingly. It was Morgan who spoke. 'It was my intention to make us known to you a little later on. The reason for calling was originally to ask for your help in tracing a J Dugdale in the parish register. I'm at a loss to explain with any great satisfaction our interest in this man. We find by chance a John Dugdale buried here and no longer desire the register search.'

'What possible concern would the police have in a very frail old man such as Mr Dugdale?' protested the vicar.

'That's just it, a good question. This person's name and that of this village were found in the possession of a man who did not die of natural causes. You understand that we must discreetly check it out. Therefore I'd be obliged if you would kindly keep this revelation totally confidential.'

'It sounds unreal – but of course!'

'What can you tell us about this man Dugdale?' Pringle asked uneasily.

'Mr Dugdale was known to me for the past 15 or 16 years. He first came to Medhurst after he'd given up work. He came to live here in retirement. He was a widower, and lived alone. A contented man at peace with the world... many hobbies and interests. He was in his late eighties when he passed on. All quite mundane, he'd been poorly for the last couple of years, and it came as no great shock when the time had come for him to meet his maker. He died in hospital – left what little he had to the church: a most kindly act.'

'More or less as I expected the circumstances might be. You'll forgive the intrusion. I can't promise that it ends here... but sincerely hope it to be the case,' Morgan concluded.

They took their leave and strolled to where they had left the car.

'You know what's next?' Morgan challenged.

'To my utter discomfort, this means we do the same in the villages of Lowplain and Denchurch.'

The inspections of the churchyards of Lowplain and Denchurch were made at a later time of day, where they could mingle with others and not be so conspicuous as they had been in Medhurst. They found in both cases the names on the list to be deceased persons. A Sloan of Lowplain matched Alice Sloan, buried this year. W Maxwell, found to be William Maxwell, also buried this year. No mysteries were attached to the perfectly normal conditions leading to the deaths of these people.

'What the hell does it all mean?' Pringle uttered in confusion.

Morgan sighed. 'I wish I knew. One buried in April, one May and one in June. Has that any significance, I wonder?'

'There's another point,' observed Pringle. 'Three on the list are dead. Fairfield, the fourth listed, is alive and kicking. Is there a chance of his life being in danger?'

'I very much doubt that. Three names are written down in order without a line space – grouped together. Fairfield's name is on its own.'

'We check out this wine shop next, do we?'

'At the appropriate time. There's an idea I must pursue before that.'

Assistant Commissioner Willoughby was as crusty as ever. 'You've not a chance in hell, Morgan, of exhumation!' he exclaimed forcefully.

'You misunderstand my meaning, sir; I have no intention of exhuming anyone. The graves are markers of some kind; that's the only thing that makes any sense to me. Places of safety – places easily found – hardly ever disturbed – can be relied upon to be always there. An ideal hiding place, in fact.'

'But not a place to be seen acting suspiciously... far too chancy.'

'Hmm. Let me put something to you that is conceivable to the criminal mind. It comes to them that the most reliable place to bury something, and perhaps, depending what it is, recover it from at a later date, is a new grave in a lonely village churchyard. They can quite easily obtain prior information on when a funeral is to take place... when one has taken place, flowers and wreaths lie on the unpacked earth: an easy place to find at night. With little effort the tributes are temporarily removed from the surface and the criminal digs and buries whatever they wish to dispose of. It's easy work, the ground is soft, they don't have to go too deeply – only a few feet at most. The tributes are then replaced. What is hidden will not be disturbed.'

'So what is it precisely you want permission for you to do?'

'I would like to be able to take a couple of men and remove one or two feet of earth from the top of one or two of those graves. It would be done at first light and be put back exactly as it was, in as little time as possible.'

'What exactly do you think you'll find?'

'I wish I knew; I hope I'm not barking up the wrong tree.' Morgan sighed. 'I can't think of any other reason why you have a list of three graves so far apart from one another, with three different names.'

Willoughby screwed up his face and shook his head violently. 'I'm apprehensive about whether I can get you that authority. You have to have a genuine reason to be given approval for that kind of action... so what, only digging down a couple of feet might not be that troublesome. In the past, some have encountered an enormous amount of objection from church authorities... I'll sound it out, see what can be done.'

CHAPTER FOURTEEN

THE WINE CIRCLE

'With all our modern technology and sophisticated equipment we don't appear to be keeping crime under control. They say that somewhere in the region of 30 deaths a week are from illegal drugs alone,' Pringle said, uncharacteristically disgruntled.

'That doesn't sound a bit like you... more like police hierarchy talking. Have you been lectured? Put under a bit of pressure?' Morgan demanded stiffly.

'Not really. Turning over in my mind a one-day seminar that I was on a while back.'

'Imagine what it would be like if we weren't already doing our best. For some it's never enough.'

The two were on their way in Morgan's car to Folly Wines & Beers, a medium-sized shop in Catford. They arrived and parked the car. They found the shop without too much effort.

As they opened the door and entered the shop, a bell sounded loudly. Assorted drinks in bottles and cans of all shapes and sizes were displayed in large circular mounds on the floor. The shop was empty of customers; no one attended the counter, but the ringing of the bell immediately brought response from the room behind.

The detectives introduced themselves and began asking questions in turn. The man behind the counter told them in reply to one that only he and his wife did the serving.

'Is your wife with you at the moment?'

'Yes, she's here. You wish to see her also?'

'Please.'

The shopkeeper fetched his wife. Pringle produced snapshots of the two Yorks and passed them across for them to look at. 'Do you recognise either of these people? Perhaps they've been into the shop. You may even know them by name.'

The two behind the counter studied long and hard. The man shook his head. 'Never seen either of them.'

'The young man, his face is familiar. I'm almost certain – though I wouldn't swear to it,' the woman said.

'Go on,' Pringle urged.

'Let me think... I vaguely remember him as the one being rather nervously awkward in putting what he wanted to say. On about his sister having been a wine enthusiast. That he needed to get in touch with some people she had known. Found our number written down by his sister. Asked if this was the place she'd got her wine from and did I possibly know her. From the description he gave, it could have been anyone. A few names were bandied about by him, but they meant nothing to me. Don't ask me the names; I couldn't recall them if I tried. I pointed out that we supply wine to a wine circle who might be able to help him, as they are enthusiasts.'

'When exactly was it he came here?'

'I couldn't rightly say exactly. The face sticks in my mind clearly now. The woman here is not familiar at all.'

'I see,' Morgan murmured with quickening interest. 'Who runs this wine circle?'

'Betty Morrison.'

'And you put this man on to her?'

'Yes, that's the best I could do for him.'

'How are you involved with this wine circle?'

'It's given us a bit of extra trade. They hire the large room upstairs over the shop. We don't live on the premises. Mrs Morrison is given the key to the side door when they need the room and returns it promptly next day.'

'Do you not attend these wine meetings yourselves?'

'We did to begin with, a few years ago, but we don't any more. It's much about the same each time. We can't grumble that they don't get all the wine from us; we do get rid of our fair share. We're more than happy with the arrangement.'

'At what time do these wine circle meetings start and finish?'

'Evenings, 7.30 till 9.30ish – perhaps even longer.'

'How often do they take place?' asked Pringle. He thought it his turn to put a question.

She turned her head slightly. 'No more than four times a year.'

Morgan took back the questioning. 'When was the last meeting?'

'Now, let me see now… um, I'll look it up and give you the exact date.'

'And also the time before, if you please.'

'I'll fetch the sales book.'

She disappeared briefly, then returned with a blue duplicate book. She laid it on the counter and flicked her way through the pages. Raising her head, she chose Morgan to give details. 'Last meeting was on the twenty-sixth of October. The one before that was on the twentieth of July.'

'Have you anything you'd like to add to what your wife has said?' Pringle inquired of the man.

The man looked put out. 'My wife has covered more than I could possibly tell you.'

'Fine... where do we find this Mrs Morrison?'

'I'll jot down her address and telephone number,' the man said helpfully, as he had contributed little beforehand.

The two detectives thanked them for their assistance and closed the door behind them.

'Wonder what all that was about!' the shopkeeper exclaimed dubiously.

'They didn't volunteer and I wasn't going to ask,' his wife retorted, unconcerned.

Morgan and Pringle accepted Mr Morrison's invitation to follow him into their cosy sitting-room.

'You have unusual visitors, Betty,' Mr Morrison announced boldly.

Betty Morrison was a very big woman with an alert, questioning face. She put down the book that she had been reading and gave them a strange stare. 'I can't see anything unusual about them,' she said with dry humour and a hearty laugh.

Her husband explained who they were.

'Oh, I see your point, dear... please make yourself comfortable, gentlemen. May I offer you some refreshment?'

'That's extremely kind,' said Morgan, 'but, thank you, no.'

She stared at them again; her raised eyebrows were enough to tell them that she was waiting for clarification.

'We have come from Folly Wines & Beers. They gave your name in connection with our inquiries.'

'Why should they have done that?' she asked eagerly. Her skin appeared to tighten and her face flushed a little. 'Nothing wrong, is there? We haven't broken the law.'

'You're not in any trouble,' Morgan assured her. 'You run a wine circle, we are told.'

'That is so: organising get-togethers for like-minded people.'

'How long have you been active in this regard?'

'When did it start, you mean? Roughly seven years ago – do you want the exact date?'

'No, that won't be necessary.'

Pringle produced the York snapshots from his pocket. 'Will you kindly take a look at these people and tell us if you recognise either of them?'

'I recognise both. I have a good eye for faces; names, however, I can't help with,' she immediately came back at him.

'It is of the utmost importance that you tell us all you know.'

She squinted. 'Are they in some sort of trouble?' she asked sharply.

'You are not aware that they are both dead? Murdered, in fact. Don't you read the newspapers?' Pringle retorted brusquely. Morgan gave him a reproachful glance.

Betty Morrison looked shocked. 'I don't like your tone of voice, young man. I avoid reading depressing things, and we don't have newspapers delivered on a regular basis any more.'

'I'm sorry, it wasn't meant to come out like that,' said Pringle.

'There was quite a write up. I must agree it's not of everyone's favourite reading,' Morgan said.

Mr Morrison cleared his throat and looked disapprovingly at Pringle. 'Surely you're not so naïve to believe that people remember everything in the news.'

'Point taken,' said Pringle.

Morgan turned his attention to Mrs Morrison. 'Tell me, please, how is it you recognise them?'

'The woman, she came one evening to one of our get-togethers. She just turned up, as so many do. Said she'd heard about us from a lady she'd spoken to. I remember she looked for her at the gathering but she didn't find her... I made her most welcome, as I do with all newcomers. She told me afterwards – when the evening finished – she had enjoyed the time spent with us. She said she would come again, but I've not seen her since – how stupid of me, if she's dead, poor woman.'

'Do you keep a register of your members?' Pringle asked in a politer tone of voice.

'We do, but not on people that come along only the once or twice. Like any society, we have people coming and going all the time. We have posters in many wine shops' windows to advertise our existence. After a few times, if they are sure they wish to become full members, they join – there's no pressure, you see, to become a member straight away. Sometimes we organise coach trips.'

'Can you remember the date she came?'

'That's easy.'

'You can remember without having to think about it? That's remarkable.'

'Not really. My brain's not that quick. It's just that I relate the time with the guest speaker. And that night it was Donald Fairfield, on the twentieth of July – a lord's son, you know! Very excited we were when he agreed to come along and give us the benefit of his wine knowledge.'

Pringle looked at Morgan; a faint smile of achievement glowed on his face.

'I've never been to a wine club, or circle as you call it, but I've heard there are quite a few up and down the country. What takes place when you have your meetings?' Morgan asked.

'It's a lot of fun. You should come along one evening. A lot of good humour and I can assure you we never drink to excess. There's naturally a fee to be paid by everyone who attends. That pays for the tasting and the hire of the room. As a group we purchase at reduced prices. It's quite informal – no formality whatsoever, just a friendly group of people with a common interest. Donald Fairfield was most interesting, I remember. Talked about a vintage wine chart. On Bordeaux... Sauternes... Rhône... Loire... Rhine... Moselle... Alsace... Champagne and Port. The châteaus in France and Château d'Yquem, the world's most sought-after wine at one time in the history of wines. He advised about the years they would be at their best from bottling. When wines were for laying down and when they were tiring and needed to be drunk. A most enlightening talk.'

'Did anyone accompany him that evening?'

'Now, let me see... yes, he introduced me to his brother, and his brother's wife – and, yes, his little sister, as he called her.'

'Was it the first time you'd met any of them?'

'Yes, that was the only time.'

'Have you ever met Lord Peter Fairfield?'

'Unfortunately not. We would have been over the moon if he'd come along.'

'What was your impression of them all?'

'Well, as I've said, Donald Fairfield was received very favourably, quite charming he was, and very entertaining.'

'And the others?'

'I wouldn't want it repeated, but his brother's wife stood out a mile; I didn't take to her at all. A proper Chloroform Jane – enough to put anyone off. Snobbish and coarse at the same time, if you know what I mean. His brother was polite and his sister rather on the quiet side. She didn't have a lot to say.'

'Did the woman in the photo sit near or speak to any of the Fairfield family, or appear to recognise any of them?'

'I know she didn't sit near them but she may have spoken to any of them in the course of the evening. We don't sit down all of the time; we do move around a bit. A party atmosphere, you see. And we have a raffle.'

'If we needed to know, would you be able to supply a register of people who attended the meeting of the twentieth of July?'

'Not exactly, no. Our regulars yes. New faces that members bring along and those that turn up on the off chance, no. Not without a lot of chasing around. And even then we may not get them all.'

'I doubt whether there will be the need. What happened when the evening broke up? This woman, did she leave on her own?'

'Let me think, yes. She thanked me for a most pleasurable time. Said she would come again and left.' Betty Morrison came to the end of the sentence in a tone that did not sound convincing. Then she added, 'She came back, though.'

'Why did she come back?'

'One of her gloves fell on the floor under the table where she'd been sitting. It was handed to me when the tables and chairs were being cleared away – you remember, darling?' she said to her husband.

'Yes,' he said, 'I remember quite well, now you've mentioned it.'

Betty Morrison continued, 'She came up and I gave it to her, and she was very pleased to get it back. That's the last I saw of her – poor dear.'

'In what order did the Fairfields leave?'

'It's been a time now, but I believe his sister went first. I remember now, she was the first to say goodnight. Then his brother and wife left, and after them Donald Fairfield. Then the woman in the photograph came back about her glove.'

'Anything else you can tell us about this woman in the photograph?'

'That's all there is, I'm afraid, apart from her buying wine she liked.'

'Now then, the man in the picture,' Pringle produced the photo again.

Betty Morrison looked at it and said, 'They're very much alike, aren't they?'

'Brother and sister,' said Morgan compassionately.

'That's pitiful – a peculiar feeling it gives me, to see their faces now that you've told me what you have.'

'Tell us all about him, if you wouldn't mind, please.'

'There's not a great deal. He called on me, and I kept him at the door. You can't be too careful these days asking strangers into one's home. He mentioned a name and asked if she was one of our members. I told him no, yet it rang a bell. I may have heard it when she introduced herself that night. Unless you see people on a regular basis, names go in one ear and out the other. He enquired about some other people. The conversation got around to our most recent meeting. I more or less told him the same as I've told you.'

'You mentioned the son of a lord to him, did you?'

'Yes, I did. Funnily enough, that's when he lost interest in what I was telling him, and he left abruptly.'

'Did you ever see him again?'

'No, that was the one and only time.'

'I wonder if you can be a little more precise than the woman in the wine shop as to the date of this young man calling on you?' Pringle asked appealingly.

'I've nothing to pinpoint it with as I had with the woman – what's her name?'

'Constance York.'

'Yes, with her. Around the end of… sorry, I can't be that sure. My guessing wouldn't help. All I can say is it was quite a time after the wine circle meeting.'

'Is there anything else you can think of? Or you, Mr Morrison?' put in Morgan tentatively.

The two Morrisons were quiet for a while, then they looked at each other. Mr Morrison shook his head, and Betty Morrison said simply, 'Nothing apart from one or two disappearing outside for a smoke on club nights.'

Morgan thanked them and cautioned them not to repeat any of the conversation that had just taken place. The two detectives then left.

Morgan looked at his companion. 'We make rapid progress, my friend. At last a pattern is shaping nicely. A Fairfield name on a bit of paper is one thing, but now we have the undisputable testimony that four Fairfields were seen in the company of Constance York. Donald, Phillip, Angela and Pamela; most promising. Any gut feeling?'

'No. I wish I had a gut feeling. "P Fairfield, Oakwood": that is what is written on the paper. Lord Peter is the only one living in Oakwood at present, and he was not one of the four attending the wine evening. On the other hand, P for Phillip was, and P for Pamela was. They both lived in Oakwood at one time. For the moment – and I know it's an old cliché – I'm happy with the newfound jigsaw pieces. More importantly, how they fit together. Do you think the Morrisons have told us all they know?'

'I can't see why not.'

'You must surely go now to the four members of the Fairfield family who attended that meeting and confront them,' Pringle said.

'You are quite right. The time is drawing ever nearer for contact with Lord P's relatives... Bear with me for a while, then I will make a start in that area. I await a development. If it turns out as I've hoped, I will be in touch, and you can be in on the final hurdle. I have not fully formulated everything in my mind; ideas at this stage, that's all. I want to avoid any wild goose chases.'

'You mustn't shut me out. You should tell me what's on your mind. If anything were to happen to you, whatever you have on your mind would be lost. I'm not very pleased concerning that. After all, I've given you everything I have,' Pringle said unhappily.

'Sorry, I should have told you before. If anything were to happen to me, my unofficial case notes and thoughts can be found in a little red book that I carry with me or keep at my home. Although we make progress, there's still the need not to be out of our depth in words and names. I must have permission to go along with my hunch at those graves. I would prefer a lot more to go on before I speak to people who will make life hell for me if I am not fully in charge of the situation. Like you, I'm not given endless time. To get it right from the very beginning is my objective,' Morgan said, determined.

CHAPTER FIFTEEN

FOURWAYS INN

Consent had been given to remove a few feet of earth from the first two graves on Morgan's list. Three men stood at the grave of John Dugdale. Stanley Jones, a burly man, with Alec Edwards, small-framed and bony-faced, and Morgan. It was first light. So early in the morning, the place had a sensitivity of both calmness and sadness. They all felt that emotion at being there at that unholy hour.

'Where would you like me to start, sir?' asked Stanley, shrugging his broad shoulders.

'I think a criminal would want a spot easy to find. Try by the headstone. Give yourself plenty of room to work in, though.' Morgan unfolded a tarpaulin and spread it on the ground. 'When you dig, put all you remove on this. It all has to go back just as we've found it,' he stressed. 'You, Alec, take photos before we start digging – particularly the name on the headstone, and also anything I'm hoping we unearth.'

'Right, governor,' said Alec obligingly, although he felt it would be a waste of time.

Stanley started digging carefully. He wasn't keen at being there, but orders were orders.

After an agonising time, Stanley said, 'I've got something. What are you, psychic?'

'Only optimism from a hunch and crossed fingers. What is it?'

'A large package, well wrapped in many layers of plastic.' Lifting it out of the grave, Stanley passed it over to Morgan.

Grabbing it with intense excitement, Morgan felt immensely relieved that he hadn't made a complete fool of himself by his guesswork. Opening the package, he was delighted in finding a quantity of smuggled drugs. 'You can't imagine how relieved I am. Someone up there is looking out for me – eureka!' he yelled, raising his voice rather loudly.

'Hush, you'll be waking the dead,' said Alec on impulse. He smiled as he remembered where he was.

'Take plenty of photos for our report,' Morgan said, still excited.

With this significant discovery, the three then drove on to the next grave in Lowplain. They had exactly the same success there. All three were in high spirits on the way back to Scotland Yard, to report on their outstanding finds.

Having so much more than he'd started with, Morgan now had to use his cunning ways with those he had to see. No disclosure would be made of the last name, W Maxwell, or of the place of Denchurch. He would speak of the brother of Constance York, found buried in woodland, and of how the investigation that followed had led to the finding of a list in the brother's place of work, surnames with the initials and small village names. One of them being P Fairfield, Oakwood. He would bring up the fact that Donald, Phillip, Angela and Pamela Fairfield had all been in the company of the later-to-be murdered Constance York. He would mention the drugs, and that there could be more discoveries of graves and more findings. That they were awaiting the outcome of a complete and thorough search at Henry York's home address for anything written down. They were hopeful of a reply in about a week. It wasn't true, but that was his plan. He knew that at this stage he was putting all his eggs in one basket.

Fourways Inn could be found a mile or so from Fairfield Manor on the right-hand side from Burbridge. Morgan felt an overnight stay there would be just what the doctor ordered. He felt weary and wanted to relax and indulge himself after all that had happened. Arriving at the inn, he drove his car into the small car park. Inside, the smell from the burning logs was quite pleasing.

The landlord, or innkeeper as some jokingly called him, was mopping up spillage from the bar top. Ben Blake loved his inn. He was a man in his mid-forties and nearly always in good humour. His accent was clearly not one of having been brought up in the city. His wife sounded very much the same when she spoke. Ben and Mary Blake had two grown-up children, John and Susan, who lived there and helped run this very old and charming thatched inn.

After Morgan had had an enjoyable meal, he booked a room for overnight. The price included a full English breakfast, served at any time between 7.30 and nine o'clock.

The night air was quite damp; the brightness from the inn's windows gave sufficient light to cross the car park with ease. After collecting his suitcase from the boot of the car, Morgan returned. A young lady of about 19 years of age – rather plump but with a very pretty face – informed him his room was ready; she would take him up. She led the way into the hall, passing a pay phone, and up one flight of stairs to a corridor where the rooms were situated.

'This one is yours, Mr Morgan,' she announced when they had reached it. 'There's clean towels, and clean linen on the bed. I've put the radiator on to warm up; you can turn it off if you don't want it. In my opinion too many improvements takes away the character of the place – don't you agree? I do hope you will be comfortable and enjoy your stay, Mr Morgan.'

'I'm sure I will, and many thanks.'

Susan Blake gave him the key to his room and departed, leaving him to unpack his overnight things and look at the interior of the room. It was, as she had said, about character. Dark wooden beams crossed the ceiling and some continued around the walls, complementing the rough white background. The furniture was old and matched perfectly. The modern wash-hand basin with mirror over the top, the shelving, the wall-to-wall carpeting, the electric lights and fittings all replaced the old jug and basin, the varnish-stained floorboards, oil lamps and candles. It had indeed altered the character. Everyone now expects modern comforts with only nostalgia remaining, he mused.

He opened his case and threw pyjamas onto the bed. Took out his shaving gear, toothbrush, toothpaste and other toilet requisites, placing them neatly on the shelves above the sink. He stripped to the waist and had a refreshing wash before going down to get his bearings.

On reaching the bottom of the stairs he turned right to follow the carpet to a part of the inn he had not seen before. Not far along the corridor was a room marked 'Lounge', and farther still were double doors that he worked out to lead to where breakfast would be taken the following morning.

The lounge was empty. Morgan ordered a glass of ale, then sat himself down in an armchair. He turned over in his mind again what had to be covered at his meetings.

Ben Blake interrupted his line of thought. 'Your drink, Mr Morgan. You'm not from round 'ere… first time, is it?' asked the landlord.

'Thank you. Yes, my first time inside your inn. I've driven past several times. I like it very much.'

'That's most kind.'

'I believe you have someone from parliament living in the vicinity,' said Morgan casually.

'Ah, you mean that Lord Fairfield, yes.'

'Does he ever show his face in here?'

'Once or twice with his brother. One of my regulars told me who they were. They seemed to get along all right to me, but gossip 'as it they don't get on all that well. Mind you, it could be only gossip; you know what some folk be like.'

'I must confess I'm not immune to a bit of gossip myself,' said Morgan with a smile.

'That makes two of us,' he chuckled.

'What about the rest of his family?'

'They could well 'ave been, for all I knows. I wouldn't recognise any of 'em. You'll have to excuse me; I'd like to stay and chat, but I must get a move on. Goodnight, sir; sleep well.' Ben Blake left, taking some empty glasses with him.

Usually, Reginald Morgan had little difficulty in dropping off to sleep once his head hit the pillow. On this particular night it was quite different to start with. He was restless as he lay in bed, wrestling with involuntary half-awake half-asleep thoughts. The moon came from behind some cloud and lit the room, casting weird shadows that made his thoughts turn to days of old. The stagecoaches en route, pulling up at this very same inn with weary, dust-covered passengers, ready for an overnight break in their journey.

97

He could almost hear the sound of wheels on gravel, tired hooves on tired horses. The country air proved in the end to be his salvation, sending him fast asleep as though he had taken sleeping pills.

Next morning he awoke early. The birds were singing. Why they sang on this grey morning he had no idea. After a wash and shave, and feeling better, he packed his case, dressed and went in search of breakfast.

On entering the dining room, he found one other guest already seated at the table, who managed a strained smile and continued chasing a reluctant sausage around his plate with a fork. Mrs Blake came bustling in to enquire what Morgan would like to eat.

After breakfast, Morgan put his suitcase in the boot of his car, locked it and set off on a short stroll through the country lanes to clear his head, in readiness for an appointment at Fairfield Manor.

CHAPTER SIXTEEN

STAFF AT THE MANOR

'This latest disclosure is quite a shock, Chief Inspector, and opposite to what I'd expected. It gives the impression of me being involved with people I've never met. Not only that, these Yorks... both dead – murdered,' Lord Peter Fairfield responded brusquely to Morgan's incriminating connecting evidence. 'I'm still in the dark. I don't know what's going on.' With a grunt, he handed back the photos and a copied list of names and places taken from the original paper.

'Keep the list; I've plenty of copies.'

'I don't know why I should want to, but I will for the time being.'

William Maxwell of Denchurch was deliberately not shown on that list. Morgan drove home the point that the original evidence was not allowed to leave police files. Peter was also given the story of the expected reply in a week's time to a request for a further search that might reveal more grave sites and drugs to be found.

Peter's normal pasty white complexion became a shade of pink. 'You have carte blanche to ask as many personal questions as you like about me to anyone. I'm as human as the next man and have weaknesses like anyone else... but murder, that's not one of them. I'm even more determined that you follow these latest findings to the full without hindrance. There's got to be an explanation – damn it – I've never even heard of the other two written on that paper. There used to be a Lord Leonard Dugdale once, but that was many years ago, in my father's time.'

Morgan was about to step in with a remark, but Peter Fairfield did not halt his flow of words long enough. 'As far as drugs are concerned, I wouldn't touch them with a barge pole. What would I need the money for? I've more than enough in my position. This is preposterous; I could retire – give up all my activities tomorrow, and still not feel the impact financially. But this is not for me, to stagnate.' He continued in a lower tone, 'With regard to the other members of the family being with that woman at the social gathering, you'll no doubt take that up with them, naturally, naturally. The family as well as myself being inexplicably involved leaves me at a loss for words. The sooner you clear up this unfortunate episode in our lives, the better. I've a lot more on my mind to think about than this sordid business.'

'Well, there it is; you now know as much as we do. I'll keep you in the picture as things progress. I'm here and must do my job, speak with the staff you have here. Show these photos, see if any of them have ever set eyes on the Yorks.'

'Be tactful, please; I dread to think of any of the staff putting in their notice because of this unsavoury business. It's very difficult finding employees that wish to live in these days, and especially in a quiet place such as Oakwood.'

'Leave it to me; I'll not antagonise anyone,' Morgan said reassuringly.

'Will you want me to call them all together or what?'

'If it's all the same to you, I'd like not to disturb them from their work, just to chat casually to them as I find them. They won't be put under any pressure. What would they be getting on with this time of day?'

100

'You have their names?'

'Yes, I've got them in my notes. Five in all at the house.'

Peter's face became a little pinker. 'Cook's – I won't score any marks for this – Cook's in the kitchen this time of day, naturally, naturally,' he said, and grinned. It was the first time Morgan had seen any sign of light-heartedness from the other man. It broke the serious-natured atmosphere that was understandable in the circumstances. Peter went on, 'Cook's daughters are around the house somewhere – light cleaning or bed making. Housekeeper's out – she shouldn't be too long. Her husband Wally is pottering outside in the garden or might be cleaning the car round the back. Feel free to do what you have to do. I'll be here working for most of the day. Please show me the courtesy of calling in on me before you leave.'

'You have my assurance, sir; that was my intention,' Morgan said.

Morgan scratched his head. It was all very well for him to think of wandering about, but he hadn't an inkling where the kitchen was situated. This came home to him in the hallway, seconds after shutting the door on the seemingly flabbergasted Lord Peter. He thought it best not to go back again until he was ready to be off.

Fortunately, the unmistakable rhythm of a vacuum cleaner met his ears from one of the rooms close by. He followed the sound and saw one of Cook's young daughters going about her task industriously. She did not hear Morgan enter because of the noise from the cleaner, but sensed his presence and looked up. She smiled sweetly at him, then turned the machine off. 'Good morning, sir; sorry about that,' she said apologetically, although there was nothing to be sorry about. 'Need any help, sir? You look a bit lost.'

Morgan looked at her uncertainly and introduced himself. 'Now, which one of Mrs Ebson's daughters are you? Is it Elsie or Freda?'

'I'm the pretty one, Freda.'

'You're not backward in coming forward.' Morgan smiled. 'This is just to see what you all look like and explain why I'm here. There are a few simple questions.'

Freda did not wait for a question. 'I suppose you want to find out if any of us are the ones making accusations about some woman and Lord Peter. I'd never do such a thing. I thought that rumour was buried and forgotten.'

'I don't think for one moment that you or any other of the staff is responsible for anything. There's a little more come to light than rumours.'

She smiled shyly; he had put her mind at ease, but not totally.

Morgan wouldn't ask questions about her employer; anything of that nature would put the young girl in an impossible situation. This was her home and her livelihood, all under one roof. How could she be expected to make comments openly, when she might feel that what she said might well get back to her employer? Instead he went through only what he wanted to be known, along with the showing of the photographs, keeping back personal details that he felt were of no consequence to the young member of staff. She appeared shocked by how much more there was to what had been gossiped about among them. When he had finished, he stated simply, 'Please don't be alarmed if you wish to tell me anything. It need only be between the two of us.'

'Oh, I wouldn't be if there were, but there isn't anything.' She gave a shake of the head and a convincing grin.

Her sister Elsie came down from upstairs and joined them. She had no misgivings on taking part in the conversation. Morgan more or less went through the same pattern as he had with Freda, ending with neither girl having set eyes on the Yorks or heard any of the names in question being mentioned in their presence.

After a short pause, he asked to be directed to the kitchen.

'You want to talk to Mum. I'll show you,' Freda Ebson said, and she led Morgan through the house to where the kitchen was situated.

'In there!' She pointed to a white painted door and discreetly went back to her sister.

Morgan tapped, did not wait for an answer and entered. Mrs Ebson stood at a worktable, her hands covered in flour. Morgan quickly took in the surroundings of the kitchen. He was no expert. Victorian or further back, he supposed, with one or two relics remaining, brought up to date with the latest equipment.

Mrs Ebson ran an eye over the stranger who had come into her domain and accepted without question who he was when he introduced himself. Then she complained disenchantingly, 'These new gadgets are a godsend, but there's some jobs that just have to be done with fingers – that's if you want things to taste as good.'

Morgan condescended, 'I've heard that view put forward by other pastry makers.' Then he said slowly, 'I've been having a pleasant chat with your daughters.'

'They were not disrespectful in any way, I hope.'

'Not in the least, quite polite.'

'As you are a detective, is it my turn to be put through the mill? To tell the truth, none of us have the time to – or want to – spread malicious untruths. You will never stop harmless gossip, but that's all it is.'

'You speak about what's going on among yourselves.'

'Oh yes, gossip spreads like runny jam... although we've had little to talk about lately. Lord Peter wouldn't be daft enough to let himself be dragged in on any type of wrongdoing.' Unexpectedly she said, 'If you want a cup of tea, make yourself useful and put the kettle on.'

Morgan obeyed, filling an electric kettle and plugging it into the socket. Mrs Ebson washed her floury hands under the tap and mustered up cups, saucers and a china teapot from the cupboard. She placed the teapot next to the kettle and put in tea bags.

At that point, Mrs Spake, the housekeeper, came in. Her lips pressed together a little tighter on her seeing Morgan. 'Oh,' she said, 'have I butted in? Sorry – I'll go.'

'No, please stay. Actually, it saves me going over things twice.'

Cook said, 'I'll pop another bag in the pot.'

When the water came to the boil she made the tea. She let it stand for a while, then began pouring. Morgan updated them on events that had brought him down to Fairfield Manor. Telling the same story over again, he felt himself already tiring of repetition. As it unfolded, they could not believe what they were hearing. The impact was overpowering.

'Incredible! I don't know what to say,' cried Mrs Ebson.

'Makes things far worse,' muttered Mrs Spake.

Morgan said softly, 'Anything at all to offer that may shed some light? Have a look at these photos.'

Mrs Ebson took command, glancing at them. 'Never seen 'em, never heard of 'em. They've not been here. That's right, isn't it, Emily? All a big mistake if you ask me. Someone makes it look black for someone and they're not involved at all. Trouble is, mud sticks no matter how innocent you are.'

Mrs Spake continued with the same premise. 'When there's talk, whether you're in the right or wrong you don't get away unscathed.'

Morgan stopped this line of chatter. 'Does Lord Fairfield get many callers?'

'Occasionally the vicar comes, and Doctor Owen – when he's not on call; likes a game of chess. Sometimes Lord Peter goes to them. That's evening time. During the day, now and then we get a guest or two for lunch... sometimes Mr French calls in to pick up documents... weekends, well, you never know. Miss Pamela mostly. Sometimes she brings a friend. Not often, but we get the odd associate of Lord Peter's calling in, sometimes they stay – it varies from week to week.'

Morgan asked, 'How about his brother and sister-in-law?'

'We see the brother from time to time but not his wife lately. I think she must be housebound – though I wouldn't dare ask.'

'And Lord Peter's other sister-in-law?'

'Haven't seen her since her sister passed away.'

'So life is not that uneventful or dull for you in the country.'

'I can't speak for everyone, but I believe we all enjoy working here,' said Mrs Spake.

'It's unthinkable, but it's got to come some day. And when that happens, it's going to be so different living here,' said Cook.

'What are you going on about, Molly?' asked Mrs Spake.

'My growing girls, of course. When they get a bit older – they'll not be here forever, you know. They'll be getting married one day. Are you married?' she asked Morgan abruptly.

'I've never got around to it somehow. It's no great catch for a woman to tie herself to a man that's hardly ever at home,' Morgan conceded reluctantly.

So far, by seeing the four domestic staff, Morgan hadn't gained much, but he had sensed a certain amount of loyalty to the man that employed them. He finished his tea, thanked them and left by a door that opened onto part of the grounds at the rear of the building.

Wally Spake was found pumping up a tyre on the inside of the garage. Morgan bade him good morning and commented on the changeable weather. Here was one of the five staff to whom the detective wanted to talk in preference. This time he would ask questions first and then give the rundown of the situation afterwards.

If anyone loved to natter, it was Wally Spake. His wife accused him many a time of being worse than any woman when it came to nattering.

Morgan said, after introducing himself, 'Have you any idea why I've come to see you?'

'None at all. We've been told of the phone call to Lord Peter, and how someone's hinted to the police that he knew – er – was involved with someone that got herself killed. He says he's being mixed up with someone else. That's the only explanation he can think of. He said if someone came around asking questions then we were to be cooperative if we could. I said to him, even if we involuntarily let slip out something innocent, that might not look too good for him. He said to talk anyway, I said, "You sure about that?" and he said, "I'm sure".'

'When Lord Peter travels any distance, you drive him; is that not so?'

'In the main, yes. Not all the time I don't. Up and down on business but not if he goes to his club or down the village. He drives himself about then.'

'Does he stay overnight sometimes, at this club?'

'It's been known.'

'And where is this club?'

'Other side of Bromley. Through the town and down the hill on the left-hand side – on the way to Catford.'

'I see... Do you keep a diary, with your driving duties jotted down?'

'Yes, I have to write things down so's I don't forget.'

'Where is your diary now?'

'In my coat, hanging over there.' He pointed.

'Would you fetch it, please? There's one or two dates you can look up that may help prove your employer is indeed being mixed up with someone else.'

Wally wiped his hands on a piece of clean rag, went to the other side of the garage to take it from his pocket and returned.

'Tell me,' said Morgan, 'what you have entered for the last day of July?' The date Morgan felt that Constance York may have stayed out all night.

Wally found the page of the thirty-first of July. 'Got it.'

'What have you entered?'

'On that date, I've got nothing written.'

'What does that mean?' Morgan said, a little agitated.

'It means I didn't drive him anywhere that day.'

'He could have used the car himself?'

'Quite possible.'

The next date Morgan gave Wally to look up was the one Henry York was understood to have met his death. But again the date was not helpful in putting Lord Fairfield completely in the clear.

107

There was one more date that Wally was given to check, the one of the wine circle meeting. The details in Wally's diary for that day showed that Peter Fairfield would have been hard pressed to have been anywhere near the area where the meeting took place.

Morgan judged it time to give Wally the recent findings on the saga, and did so. The extra connection of the York name and the mention of drugs being somehow linked to the man Wally worked for left him floundering.

'Strewth! It's far worse than I'd bargained for. It's too complicated for the likes of me. Full of twists and turns like a maze of rabbit warrens, going in all directions.'

'You've driven the man around; dwell on the faces and names. Something later may ring a bell in your subconscious and help Lord Peter. Please give it some thought.'

'You can count on it,' said Wally earnestly. 'But I don't know if there's anything in my subconscious to ring any bells.'

'Thank you; do your best. You can finish blowing up that tyre now.'

'With my luck, I'll run out of air,' grumbled Wally.

Morgan returned to Lord Fairfield, who looked at the detective questioningly.

'Well?'

'As expected, they all appear completely in the dark. They have, in my opinion, a great deal of loyalty toward you.'

'That's nice to hear... very nice to hear.'

'I now undertake calling on the rest of your relations. In particular the ones seen in the presence of the York woman. As I said, I'll keep you posted, if I can, on any notable findings, good or otherwise. I have a feeling they're not going to greet me with open arms.'

'They'll just have to put up with it!' Peter Fairfield exclaimed, not very sympathetically, and with a hardening of voice.

CHAPTER SEVENTEEN

THE FAMILY

Morgan had to make a start somewhere with the Fairfield family. He would make that start on the two sisters-in-law of Lord Peter, he decided. One of them lived in Oakwood, the other at Kew. The one at Kew was the sister to the late Lady Fairfield – and staying with her was Pamela Fairfield. That was where he would begin. The call would be made whilst Pamela was at work. It would be better that way. Some were less inhibited and spoke more freely on a one-to-one basis.

The house in Kew was situated in a back street, not far from the well-known Kew Gardens. Morgan found the address easily. Sarah welcomed him in after he introduced himself. She was a tall woman with untidy brown hair.

'Your name sounds familiar. You've met my niece, haven't you?' she asked.

'Yes, we've spent a bit of time together,' he replied.

'If you want her now, she's at work, I'm afraid.'

'No, it's you I've come to see. I'll speak to Pamela some other time,' Morgan said.

Her voice sounded a bit croaky. 'You'll have to forgive my crackling voice – I've a bit of a sore throat.'

'Would you prefer I called another time? When you're feeling better,' suggested Morgan.

'That won't be necessary, just a bit of a chill – perhaps a cold coming on.'

Morgan went through the circumstances from the beginning. She listened quietly throughout his story, occasionally clearing her throat by lightly coughing into a small, dainty, inadequate handkerchief. There came no outrageous outburst of indignation in response. Her face was pleasant yet expressionless.

'That is a remarkable story. I don't know why you are telling me all this. I'm not involved with any of it. Pamela told me snippets about the phone call and the letter. You've added enormously to what I've heard. All very scary – not nice to hear. There has to be a rational explanation, surely. I haven't been to Oakwood since my sister passed away. After all, the Fairfields are only family by marriage. I've no knowledge of the people you speak of, or seen the two in the photos.'

'Do you believe your brother-in-law or any other of your relations are capable of being involved with drugs and murder?'

'Peter's no saint, but drugs and murder is ludicrous,' she said wheezily.

'I get the feeling you're not over-fond of him.'

'You'd be entirely wrong. I do not dislike my brother-in-law.'

'I hear in the past – in his younger days – Peter Fairfield was a bit of a ladies' man – perhaps still is.' Morgan took a chance with an outlandish shot in the dark: 'Perhaps you felt he was deceiving your married sister when she was alive. You feel he may have let her down.'

Morgan was not at all sure why he had started to get personal, as he had with Mr Biley – or was he trying to provoke her into letting something slip? Things on his mind

111

came out involuntarily at the oddest times and he was vexed for not keeping them to himself.

'Although Peter was married to my sister, I believe he may not always have been entirely faithful to her. I have no proof, just hearsay. For your ears only, Peter tried, on one occasion only, to get a little fresh with me – not forcefully, I assure you. He didn't force his attention – it was petty judging by today's standards and hardly worth mentioning. He's nice enough really, but in that department perhaps a little weak. He may have been drinking at the time, for all I know – but he didn't seem drunk.'

Morgan was pleased by how easily she had come out with this disclosure.

'I rarely see Peter these days. Harriet only sees him when he calls at his brother's house. She's not in the best of health and doesn't get about like she used to. There's no animosity on my part, so don't repeat anything I tell you.'

'I won't,' said Morgan.

Pamela's aunt turned the subject to her niece. 'Pamela stays with me to be near her work. It's a harmonious arrangement. She's a lively girl – a bit wild, perhaps, but no bother. Out for best part of the time. Very considerate when she comes in late, and lets me know if she's staying with a friend or at the manor. I won't have bad feelings – not after all this time.'

'Personal things you tell me are strictly confidential, I assure you. Your brother-in-law placed no restrictions on my asking personal questions about him; in fact, he encouraged it, if it cleared him in other respects. There's two sides to every coin. Pamela doesn't say anything about you not seeing much of the family?'

'No, why should she? Not to go visiting is understandable. Families do drift apart over the years – nothing unusual in that. As I've said, I'm only related to the

Fairfields by marriage, after all. I don't want this to be taken the wrong way… you can pick your friends, but you can't choose your relations.'

'That's very true. Have you no car of your own?'

'I did up until the end of summer. I found it rather an expensive luxury because for most of the time it stood idle outside the house. It's fine if you have need of one on a regular basis, but I hardly used the thing. What with the price of petrol, road tax, the insurance, servicing, parking meters and MOT, pays me to go by taxi when I need to go anywhere. Pamela's offered to drive me many times.'

'Are you in close contact with others in the family apart from Pamela?'

'Very minimal. The odd phone call now and then.'

'Will you tell me what your feelings are towards your nephews Phillip and Donald, and their wives? I've yet to make myself known to them on the matter related earlier.'

'I'm surprised you didn't go to them instead of me.'

'To be perfectly honest, you were the nearest. And I wanted your opinions. Can you fill me in on what they are like?'

She considered his words thoughtfully for a moment, then decided speaking of someone other than herself would do no harm. 'I see little of them; they're both busy men. Angela keeps Phillip under her thumb, so I believe. It would pay him to be a bit more of a man and put his foot down. I think she's an embarrassment to him that he could well do without. She's so sanctimonious; she ridiculed Liz – behind her back – said she was three strawberries short of a punnet. That wasn't very nice. Pamela hates her guts. Quite the other way round with Donald and Liz. Donald can charm the birds from the trees when he wants to, but lacks understanding. Liz is a run-of-the-mill sort of a person. Donald shows her up in company at times, so I hear – I don't like that sort of thing. I'm surprised she is still with him. I wouldn't put up with it.'

'Any disagreement with any of them?'

'No, I don't get mixed up in their affairs. I don't have much chance with only the odd phone call. No, I never interfere, but I do listen to what Pamela tells me about what's going on.'

'Can you tell me a little of Peter's brother, Edgar, and of his wife? Anything – anything at all.'

'We always got on very well – nice couple. You'll have to please excuse me; my throat is becoming quite sore. I'm going to make myself a hot lemon drink.' She got up from where she sat and politely beckoned him to the door. He made no attempt to dissuade her.

'Sorry I've kept you so long. Kindly tell Pamela that I will be in touch as soon as I can,' Morgan said finally.

'I will; it's a pity that it's not under better circumstances.'

Edgar and Harriet Fairfield's cottage was nowhere near on the grand scale of Fairfield Manor. It was, however, an extremely nice property. They employed just one woman who came daily. It was the daily help who opened the door to Morgan. She was roughly 50, with wispy grey hair. She left Morgan waiting at the front door while she tottered off inside to make his arrival known. Edgar Fairfield's stocky figure with round jovial face and bald forehead appeared swiftly and invited him in.

Harriet Fairfield sat by the fire in the drawing room. She looked at Morgan as he entered. 'Please excuse me not rising; I'm not an invalid, but some days my rheumatism plays me up more than others.'

'Please, that's quite all right; it must be very painful.'

114

Edgar sat down in the other armchair by the fireside and made signs for Morgan to be seated on the settee.

'Poor Peter,' Edgar said. 'We've heard the latest.'

'It doesn't take long to get about,' Morgan emphasised.

'Both Peter and Sarah phoned,' announced Harriet openly.

'Is there anything you wish to tell me?'

'What can we possibly tell you? We are as mystified as Peter. The phone call, the accusation, now his name on a bit of paper – it is his name – I mean, how many P Fairfields are there in Oakwood? And the drug thing – and the woman attending the same function as family, and the dead brother. We have nothing helpful for you, I'm afraid,' Edgar said feebly.

'There are just a few questions to put to you both. Sorry if they are personal.'

'If it's of any use, we will try to answer them,' Harriet said.

'Have either of you been separated in the last four months? Spent periods apart for any length of time?'

'No, we are always together. I'm home every night – every night regular,' said Edgar adamantly.

'You agree, Mrs Fairfield?'

'I most certainly do – I'd be helpless left on my own – and he wouldn't lie. I don't understand.'

'Sorry, I had to ask. Have you only the one car?'

'Only the one; my wife does not drive,' Edgar replied flatly.

To be positive that Edgar and Harriet had all the correct information to sink in, Morgan spent some time going over every detail as he had with the others. Thereby being certain of producing the effects he so desired. The fact that they were phoning one another with parts – if not all – of his narrative was music to his ears.

Phillip and Angela Fairfield received him coldly. Angela was full of indignation. 'So you've finally got round to us, have you? You have no right to allow servants access to such personal details. It is unthinkable of you. Most irresponsible. I don't know what the country's coming to. I'll write to your superior if it should happen again. We are not without influence, you know,' she burst out angrily.

Morgan retorted, 'You'll find I have every right, madam; murder cannot be taken lightly. In any case, I don't think the staff would class themselves nowadays as servants. Domestic staff, yes.'

She glared at him venomously. 'No, they're given too many privileges – not kept in their place as they used to be.'

Morgan ignored her and turned to Phillip, producing the photos of Constance and Henry York. 'What can you tell me of these two?' he asked bluntly.

Phillip looked at them and then to his wife. She snatched the snaps from him, gave a quick glance and handed them back to Morgan. She took it upon herself to answer for both of them. 'Complete strangers,' she said uninterestedly.

'Complete strangers, you say, and yet you spent hours together in the same room on the evening of the twentieth of July with the woman in the photograph. Come now, you can do better than that. You recall going to Catford to a wine circle meeting.'

'Okay, so what if we did? We still don't know her,' she sneered.

'My wife is quite correct; we might have to admit that her face is familiar, but she's a complete stranger – and so is the man. He wasn't there.'

'So you noticed her but not him?'

'Yes, all right, but nothing more than that.'

'He never tried to make contact with either of you?'

'No, he did not,' said Phillip.

'Or you, Mrs Fairfield?'

'Certainly not!' she said firmly and abrasively.

'What if I were to suggest that the "P" on that incomplete list is for Phillip and not Peter?'

Phillip stroked his moustache. 'I appreciate that you have a job to do, Chief Inspector, and the police have always my support, but you are way off in thinking that I have anything to do with any of this. And, as a small matter may have escaped you, let me point out that I have not lived in Oakwood since my marriage, and that's the place written after the name.'

'I thank you for your support of the police. And I do appreciate the point you make, which had not escaped me… I noticed two cars outside; you both drive?'

'We do. Nothing wrong in that, is there?' Angela remarked sourly.

'Nothing at all… Are you away much on business, Mr Fairfield?'

'Some of the time, yes.'

'And you stay here on your own while he's away, Mrs Fairfield?'

'Naturally. What are you implying?' she said with a smirk on her face.

'I imply nothing, madam. You have no fear of being in a house of this size on your own?'

She thrived on being called 'madam', wallowing in her self-importance. 'None; it's not in my make-up to be frightened of anyone.'

Every little detail that had come to light was given to them.

'Can you give any explanation as to why the name of P Fairfield of Oakwood was found in the possession of a murdered man, written down by the woman – also murdered – that four of you spent time with?' emphasised Morgan.

'It's as much of a mystery to us as it is to you. You're the detective; that's what you're paid for,' Phillip answered authoritatively.

Leaving them, Morgan hoped they would stew on all he had spoken of. He thought to himself, what a hateful woman to be married to.

'Let me point out to you, Inspector,' replied Donald Fairfield amiably, 'that I've no axe to grind in this matter. None of us had anything to do with the organising of that wine party. I was contacted and asked if I would like to give a talk of my choice on any part of the wine trade. I accepted. As I thought it unlikely me knowing anyone at this party, I asked Phillip and Pamela to come along. Angela didn't want to be left out and joined us. I didn't want Angela to come along, but that's the way she is. If I had turned down the invitation, none of us would have been there that night.'

'Agreed, but that doesn't explain all the other co-instances.' Morgan turned to face Liz, whose eyes were keenly staring at him. 'You did not wish to go with your husband that evening, Mrs Fairfield?'

Donald answered for her. 'She's no interest in wines.'

Liz said, 'I had a friend once that—'

Donald broke in. 'You and your friends. I'm sure the inspector doesn't have the time to hear about that, Liz.'

Morgan said, 'If it would help me, I'd be only too pleased.'

'I was simply going to say – if you'd let me finish – but you never do let me finish,' Liz said coldly. 'Forget it!'

'Sorry, didn't want to waste time,' Donald said.

'Can you remember in what order the four of you left the party?' Morgan asked Donald.

'I'm not sure; I couldn't be that positive whether it was Phillip and Angela first, or Pamela. I know that they left before I did. I wasn't paying that much attention.'

'When you did finally leave, do you remember passing that woman in the street? She was on her way back to retrieve her glove.'

'I faintly recall a woman; I wasn't interested who it was. What's all this about? Surely you don't suspect me, after what I've told you.'

'It is my duty to cover all avenues; there's nothing personal. What did you do after that?' Morgan asked.

'Drove home.'

'Where were you parked?'

'A long way from the entrance. It's not easy finding a parking spot.'

'Anything else to mention after you left the meeting on your way to the car?'

There was a longer pause than seemed necessary, Morgan felt, before Donald gave the answer: 'Nothing of any importance.'

'How many cars have you?'

'Only the two, mine and Liz's.'

'Mine's the small blue one,' Liz said.

'You must be very busy this time of year, Mr Fairfield.'

'Very busy indeed.'

'Are you away many nights in your profession, sir?'

'It is one of the drawbacks of my trade; I am regularly away in the wine-producing regions.'

'What do you feel about that, Mrs Fairfield?'

'I'm not overjoyed about it,' she said despondently. But truthfully she couldn't have cared less. Her husband was agreeable to strangers and in business, but he could be at times a very cantankerous man.

'Would it surprise you to learn, Mr Fairfield, that the man in the photograph made enquiries at Mrs Morrison's home about his sister's acquaintances? And that after being told about Lord Peter's son giving a talk at that meeting, he seemed to have found what he was looking for, and made no further demands on her and went away? Now, this is most important: did this man Henry York make contact in any way, shape or form?'

'No, emphatically not!'

'Or anyone else on his behalf?'

'The only unwanted calls that come to mind are the ones received way back at the end of June, when some idiot phoned here on a couple of occasions, and each time I answered there was a lull before whoever it was on the other end hung up. I got quite annoyed.'

'How about you, Mrs Fairfield? Has anyone ever turned up on the doorstep or phoned asking for your husband that you didn't recognise?'

She shook her head thoughtfully. 'I would have remembered if they had. Donald's not at home a lot of the time and I answer most of the calls. Of course we have people asking for him, mainly to do with the buying and selling wine.'

Morgan went through again all that had been found, emphasising the copy of the list of names and mentioning the expected information from the dead man's home.

After Morgan had gone, there was an uneasy atmosphere between them. Liz said, 'You didn't tell him everything about the night of the wine party, Donald.'

'Look here, Liz, I only tell people what I think is important. Why say more than is necessary?'

Pamela Fairfield made an appointment and called in at New Scotland Yard after work. She preferred it that way.

'It is most kind of you to come,' Morgan said gratefully. He took in her young, attractive, slender appearance. 'Nice to see you again.' He wasn't so sure now whether he was being hoodwinked by her, after all the new revelations. Could any of them be trusted to tell the truth?

'I'm sorry we have to meet again under these circumstances. For my father's sake I'm deeply shocked and saddened at what I heard. I can't believe what you have uncovered since our night at the theatre. To hear now that I was with the woman that Dad was accused of being on friendly terms with is mind-boggling. I had no idea when I asked to see you that night.'

Morgan said, 'With all that has come to light, I'm afraid there's more to it than just an accusation. I must say, you are the only one I've spoken to who appears to have any concern for your father's feelings.'

'I wouldn't know about that − Dad's always been very good to me. As far as the rest of the family goes, there's always bickering.'

'You are a pretty girl, and I hope wise enough never to get yourself mixed up with drugs. Those that go clubbing are often at risk.'

'I'm a woman, and don't go clubbing. I've no intention of being led down that road.'

'I am pleased to hear it. Yes, you are a woman. I'm sorry, this is the second time you've had to rebuke me.' He grinned. 'The dangers there are if they're used other than for medication.'

'Don't you think I know that? I'm not involved.'

Morgan went through again all he had covered with the others; he then asked, 'What if I were to tell you that the

121

"P" on that piece of paper is not for Peter or Phillip, but for Pamela? I don't like having to say that, but it's an option.'

She looked at him directly in the eyes. 'You are considering the three choices. I'd say you are wrong even to consider me, but I know you have to. If I were in your shoes I'd be doing the very same thing.'

Morgan glanced back at her amusedly. The photographs of the two Yorks were truly well viewed by now, and Pamela's comments were little different from those previous.

'No attempt was made by this Henry York to contact me, and I've never seen him,' Pamela said.

'As you were at this meeting of wine enthusiastic people, can you tell me anything that might be of help?' Morgan asked.

'Donald asked me if I wanted to go along, and I did. I wouldn't have gone if I'd known Angela would be there. I saw that York woman. We spoke only a few words to one other; that was when I was next to her and we remarked on the taste of a certain wine. That was it. We moved apart again and on to something else. When I got bored, I went. I don't know what more there is to say.'

'Do you think John French will be taken into your father's confidence regarding why I called on him again?'

'I expect John will; everyone else knows. There's no reason to keep anything back from him. He must have been down at the manor near enough the same time as you were there on that day. Father told me about your visit and of speaking to John a little while afterwards. I'm surprised you didn't see him.'

'I may well have passed him on the road out of Oakwood, as he was driving in.'

CHAPTER EIGHTEEN

ODDS AND ENDS

Morgan sat by a cheerful fire at his home, going over his notes. He had not long returned. The clock on the mantelpiece struck ten.

Although Morgan lived alone he never allowed himself to let standards fall. On his way home he had called in for takeaway fish and chips for his supper. He laid his place at the table tidily with the same care as if company were expected, then moved the food from its paper wrapping onto a warmed plate. Some on their own might not have taken the same trouble, instead eating straight from the paper. He looked at the fillet of fish and reflected on Peter Fairfield's experience in Corfu. Would a man concerned about a fish be capable of murder? he pondered. After the meal, he washed the dirties and put the crockery neatly away.

In the quiet of his home, there were a few scraps of information that he had to give some thought to. Information in the sense of other names that had crept in during the inquiries. There were far too many names for his liking that had accumulated since he had first opened the file on Constance York – and putting faces to names on paper never turned out as imagined. He had no intention of seeking anyone connected with Lord Peter Fairfield's political or business affairs for now, giving himself the satisfaction of not having to deal with the enormity that that would entail. As things stood at the moment, there were no circumstances to suggest such figures were involved.

Basil Broadwater, Mary Austin and Joan Tyler were three names listed as guests on a few occasions at the Fairfield home. At this juncture, he ought not to waste time on them. It could cause dismay and bewilderment, making the situation for Pamela Fairfield awkward, if they were told unnecessary details. He did not consider it convincing or profitable to make himself known to them. He hoped he was not wrong.

There were the doctor, the vicar, Fairfield's club members and any other Tom, Dick or Harry. The consideration of all that work made him downhearted. His team at Scotland Yard had discreetly found out quite a lot of personal details about some of the Fairfield family members. Whether that would be of any use he did not know. He gave up further thoughts and went to bed.

Next morning, Morgan opened his eyes before the alarm clock at his elbow had time to go off. He raised his head to look at the time, breathed a sigh of relief, gently lowered his head back onto the pillow and relaxed for another ten minutes.

He got out of bed and covered his pyjamas with a dressing gown. The room was not warm, but that was how he liked it to be. He had never been a one for central heating. Time spent in hotel rooms with that form of heating gave him a headache. He was, however, happy to have the luxury of the heat from an electric fan heater in the bathroom. After a visit there he dressed, yawned and made himself a pot of tea. Breaking two eggs into a saucepan, adding a knob of butter, salt and pepper, and a small amount of milk, he proceeded to whip up scrambled eggs over a low heat with a wooden spoon until firm.

As he ate, he listened to the radio. There was no blackout to the news media in force regarding the discoveries made in the graveyards of Medhurst and Lowplain. He was pleased they had not been held back. The more they were advertised, the better.

Half an hour later Morgan was on his way in the car, full of expectation that his plan was gradually coming together. He truly hoped it would work.

CHAPTER NINETEEN

WHICH OF THEM

Margaret Williams ushered Inspector Pringle into Morgan's private room at New Scotland Yard. They greeted one another warmly.

'You were able to swing it, then – me being under your wing for a couple of days and nights,' Pringle said dutifully.

'Under the circumstances, not a problem. The powers that be – and myself – are more than grateful for the part you and your Sussex team have contributed on the York case. You have been informed of the drug finds. They alone more than compensate for the expense and running around. It's not over yet. It's make or break for my little scheme. If it brings a result I'd like you to be in on it as you deserve. I'll fill you in as we go along.'

'More of living under a cloud,' Pringle said jokingly.

'Not quite,' replied Morgan, with a smile.

Pringle seized on what was uppermost in his mind. 'I am anxious to hear what the Fairfields at the wine gathering had to say for themselves.'

'I know you wanted rapid action over that, but in my judgment I left them till last. I dare say you feel I'm a bit of a dodderer, but in my younger days I jumped in with my size nines and that wasn't the right thing to do. I'll run through what I've been up to since our last meeting.'

'I'm all ears,' Pringle said.

'I phoned Lord P, who agreed to receive me and had no objection to my speaking to the staff at his home. He had no idea of what I had in store for him at that time.' He cleared his throat. 'As my appointment with him was for the following day, I motored down and booked a room for an overnight stay at Fourways Inn. I can recommend the place.'

'All right for some,' Pringle said, dryly.

'It was not on expenses. I treated myself. Apart from that, we met up the following day; I showed Lord P a copy of your list of names and explained the subsequent finding of the graves, carefully leaving out the last name and place on that list. The mention of drugs and the fact that four of his family members had actually been with the woman he had been accused of being on friendly terms with, and who had been murdered, left him in an outward state of devastation. Or at least that was the impression he gave. He didn't care who I spoke to or what I revealed as long as I could put an end to the mounting implications.'

Morgan stopped, got up from his chair, went to the window and looked down thoughtfully at the traffic for a few moments, then sat himself down again.

'Is he as innocent as he professes?'

Morgan stroked his chin. 'A few points to think on: he has a large car. During the working day, he's driven around by a man called Wally Spake. He drives himself about when on social pastimes. Now and again he stays at his club all night, or he could be somewhere else and prefer others to believe that's where he's been. I've nothing to go on in saying that; just a thought. The club's in Bromley, by the way. Henry York was temporarily staying in Bromley, a stone's throw from the wine shop in Catford, and no great distance from Croydon where Constance York lived. All in close proximity. Has that any substance? Lord P is well-to-

127

do and successful. To be mixed up in the distribution of drugs to addicts is pointless. Equally pointless is whether he wants female company, even of the pay-to kind; if he does, what of it? He's a widower, and what he does is of no great value or interest to anyone, apart from a little embarrassment. The most we can theorise about him is that he is protecting someone – his daughter, for instance. Or pretending to be the victim to avoid suspicion. I'm not convinced by that line of thinking.'

'There's a lot of angles,' said Pringle. 'This case is incredibly complex. For all we know there could be more than one of 'em in on it.'

'True. But I have reservations as to more than one being responsible for the two murders. I may be quite wrong. As to the staff down there, I had no expectations of getting much out of them, but I spread the gospel as intended and got a little from Wally Spake. On the whole, a jolly good-natured lot, his employees.'

Pringle made no comment and waited for Morgan to carry on.

'From my visit to Oakwood, I called on Peter Fairfield's sister-in-law who lives in Kew, a Miss Sarah Appleby. Among other details I learned was that she drove a car up to and beyond the time of Henry York's death. She gave me good reason for parting with it, but was it the real reason, I wonder?'

'You're not happy it was coincidental?' queried Pringle.

'Some kind of vehicle would have been needed to take the body of Henry York to the woodland unless he was actually killed there. You can't take a dead body by bus or train – now can you?' Morgan smiled cheerfully. 'And how convenient having no car to be gone over by the police if it had been used in the transportation.'

'By the sound of it, you are not limiting suspects to one of the four I'm waiting to be told about.'

'To begin with, when we had no idea of motive, it could have been anyone, but now, knowing what we do and with confidential checks made on all those I've seen, I believe the staff at Westminster and Oakwood to have had no part in it. Nor his business or political associates. That reduces the number to start with. As far as others, I must keep an open mind. I really hope I'm not wrong in dismissing all those people.'

'And be prepared for the unforeseen and disappointment,' Pringle offered cautiously.

'I'm pinning my trust that we won't have to wait too long for the truth.'

Morgan went on to relate the whole of the interview with Miss Appleby in detail. Then he said, 'Just because someone tells you something, you can't for certain accept it as being the truth. Sometimes it's the exact opposite. For example, what if what Sarah Appleby said about Peter Fairfield's advances to her were the other way round, and it was she who made advances to him, and he did not respond... I've no intention of following that up, but you never know, do you? And it is not of any use. All I'm pointing out is, you can't believe all you're told.'

Margaret Williams came in with some urgent papers to be signed. After that had been attended to, Morgan took up where he had left off: 'Now, where was I? Ah, yes, from Miss Appleby, I made a call at the home of Edgar Fairfield. Having seen and spoken to him and his wife, I can't bring myself to entertain the thought of either of those two getting mixed up in drugs trafficking and murder, but stranger things have happened; you never can be sure; sweet old ladies do make the best arsenic poisoners. Edgar is not in the same league as his brother and some believe he is inwardly jealous of him. So much has been bandied about, it's difficult to know what to believe half the time. One thing that struck me was the deep voice Harriet has. A voice well suited for making phone calls where the recipient would have difficulty knowing whether the caller be male or female. But, naturally, Lord P would have recognised whose voice it was. That she has probable equipment for making anonymous calls having been said, she's hardly the person for striking a heavy blow and hauling a dead body through woodland. I know Henry York was of small build but she's not capable on her own. I've had her condition confirmed; I wouldn't ask her doctor – he wouldn't tell me anything if I asked – but there are ways and means, and she does suffer quite badly from a rheumatoid complaint. That's not to say that they are not both in it; according to them they spend no time apart and he's capable physically.'

Pringle said frantically, 'Put me out of my misery and tell me what Donald, Phillip, Angela and Pamela Fairfield had to offer when you tackled them.'

'Ah, now, all in good time. As it happens, my very next call was on Phillip and Angela Fairfield.'

'At last,' drawled Pringle, with some delight.

'And I can tell you, this particular Mrs Fairfield,' groaned Morgan, 'is one of the most overbearing women I've ever came across. The meeting was hard going. They flatly denied any knowledge of the Yorks on seeing the photos. When I pointed out they'd been in the same room for two hours or more with the woman, they had to admit to perhaps having noticing her. I persisted, pointing out that the P on that list might be for Phillip and not Peter. I emphasised the position that Henry York had found himself in when given the information from Mrs Morrison, and reasoned with them that Henry would surely have tried to make contact with one of the Fairfields that had been with his sister that night. They emphatically said no one had tried to get in touch with them. By the way, Phillip's business is hardly thriving at the moment, with the uncertainty in the property development market. I don't believe he would refuse a windfall. When things were booming, it was a different matter; they liked to gamble. Lost a lot, I hear. They can't afford to do that now; he's in need of money in his line of work. Had to pull their horns in a bit. Living the way they do doesn't come cheap... would a man like that be tempted when things got rough? It's likely to be many years before he will get any of his father's money. Although I wouldn't be surprised if Lord Peter hadn't bailed him out once or twice in the past.'

Pringle said, 'Amazing what can be uncovered about people when you start to dig.'

'We'd never get anywhere in our profession if that wasn't part of our makeup.'

'And Donald and Pamela? What did they have to say about it all?'

'Donald Fairfield, ah yes. What I've heard about him being charismatic, I'm not too sure that's true. More or less the same story with him: never heard of the Yorks, no axe to grind, may have laid eyes on her during the evening. I asked other questions and saw his wife's face from the corner of my eye, and noticed funny looks she gave him. It occurred to me that drugs could be easily smuggled in his type of business from abroad. Perhaps false sections in the wine barrels. These drug barons and their muck spreaders are getting cleverer all the time in concocting new ways of fooling customs so they can shift the stuff into receptive countries.'

'He's open to be a distinct suspect, is he?'

'I had a very strong suspicion to begin with. This time of year in his trade, there shouldn't be any lack of funds...

131

unless of course there were earlier money problems that we were unable to find out about. I come again to the question of what Henry York did after Mrs Morrison had given him the Fairfield name. Henry must have been very pleased with his amateur detective work at that moment. I asked both Donald and his wife if Henry York or anyone else on his behalf had tried to get in touch with them. They said nobody had. Then Donald called to mind something that happened back at the end of June, when he had answered the phone on a couple of occasions, and the one on the other end remained silent and put the phone down on him each time.'

'Is that significant?'

'Too far back, isn't it? I was more interested in Henry following up on his information. One or more of them are lying. One of them was contacted and one of them killed him; that's what I firmly believe.'

'With that in mind, you've given thought to where they all were at the time of Henry's death, no doubt.'

'That's what's so disconcerting; any of them except Donald could have had opportunity and been responsible for Henry's death. That is to say, they were in the country. Donald wasn't; he was in France at the time, on a visit to two or three vineyards. Unless, of course, he could have jetted over and back speedily – which is most unlikely. I felt I might have got somewhere with him.'

'And Pamela Fairfield, what did you make of her? What did she have to say for herself?'

'Strange as it may seem, I didn't have to go searching for Pamela. She came here. Sat in that very chair you are sitting in now. To cut a long story short, her answers were slightly different from the rest; she recognised the York woman and briefly spoke to her. She gave this information freely; didn't have to squeeze it out of her.'

Pringle's eyes sparkled. 'Ah now, that's interesting.'

'Sorry to disappoint you; it was only to comment on the taste of one of the wines, nothing more.'

'Shame. And you believe that's all there was to it?'

'I've nothing to prove otherwise... there are so many angles, as you rightly say. The criminals have to do nothing apart from their crimes, but we have it all to do, finding indisputable evidence to obtain a conviction. That's how it is – as well you know. So then, there you are: the Fairfield bunch; take your pick.'

CHAPTER TWENTY

END IN SIGHT

It was dark, cold and eerie. Pringle and Morgan stood hidden in shrubbery with a clear sight of the grave of William Maxwell. The two men were well wrapped up in warm clothing and had prepared for a long wait by bringing flasks of hot coffee. They'd also brought with them two light foldaway chairs.

'This can't be kept up forever; do you believe this is going to work?' Pringle asked in hushed tones.

'If it doesn't, I'm running out of options... I know one thing: I'd like a smoke to break the boredom.'

'That's right out. Would give the game away.'

'Oh, I know I can't. We'd also be a couple of idiots hiding here if one of us had a coughing and sneezing fit,' said Morgan.

The village clock struck two. It was some 20 minutes or so after that that a car's engine was heard coming in the direction of the out-of-the-way church. The lone person in the vehicle switched off the engine, freewheeled almost noiselessly down the slope and stopped by the stone wall of the churchyard. The two detectives hardly dared breathe. Morgan whispered, 'Get your torch at the ready, but for Pete's sake don't turn it on till we're sure.'

They heard the sound of movement; the gentle raising and lowering of a car boot. Then the wait.

The eyes of the two men had accustomed themselves and adjusted well to the moonlight. Their ears attuned to the slightest sound. They made out plainly the shape of a figure which moved across in front of them. After a little hesitation, the image proceeded to the grave that had been under continuous observation ever since Morgan had uncovered drugs in the other two. The indistinguishable figure wore a trilby hat and a long-length overcoat, turned up at the collar, with a scarf half covering the face. A light ladies' garden spade was carried in the right hand, and a smaller object in the left.

Aware not to move a muscle, the two in the shrubbery waited patiently and in complete silence. The digging began. Pringle thought to himself, how could anyone be so totally unconcerned as to come along to a place like this and desecrate another's resting place? How absolutely appalling. But he was seeing it for himself, there, right in front of him. The digging continued and Pringle shuddered.

At last it was coming to a head. All of Morgan's hopes and optimism had been pinned on that choice. He more than once had wondered dismally whether anyone as clever and as cunning as the murderer of the Yorks would fall for his simple deception. He had banked on money outweighing common sense and that caution would be thrown to the wind – and it had proven to be so. All his conniving and endless running around being worthwhile in the end.

The waiting seemed endless, then they saw being retrieved, in the hand of the digger, the familiar-to-Morgan plastic-covered large package.

'Now!' whispered Morgan spontaneously, with all the adrenaline flowing. The two rushed forward shining their torches on the surprised figure, now enraged and looking as awesome as Count Dracula beside the disturbed grave.

'Stay where you are! We are police officers,' shouted Pringle. Being the younger man, he reached the graveside slightly ahead of Morgan.

The grotesque, trilby-hatted figure's hands made no move for the garden spade that stood upright in the ground, but as if by magic brandished the other item it had carried into the graveyard. It was a short length of metal pipe, with wood running through the centre and out at one end, roughly handle-shaped – a homemade deadly cosh.

Pringle let out an almighty cry of agony as the cosh came violently down upon his arm. His torch fell to the ground. Morgan lurched forward and grabbed the wrist that held the weapon. Pringle, although in terrible pain, retrieved his torch with his good arm and shone it on the struggling pair.

Morgan was relieved to find his opponent less powerful than surmised. The surge of strength and defiance was one of realisation and anger of being found out, and not as artful as believed. Coming to terms with that would be unbearable.

Morgan easily gained the upper hand and wrenched off the trilby hat. Long blonde hair fell down around a hostile face. The London detective gasped when he saw who it turned out to be; the face belonged to Elizabeth Fairfield. She swore, ranted and raved; an amazing conglomeration of unladylike words flowed from her lovely lips. All self-control had gone. She screamed more abuse and attempted to kick out at Morgan, but he was too quick and avoided the impact of her foot. Throwing her onto the freshly dug earth, he handcuffed her.

Leaving the churchyard, all three were feeling varying degrees of discomfort. Morgan called for an ambulance. An incident team took over to photograph and record events. Elizabeth Fairfield was formally charged and taken away.

Pringle went immediately to hospital for treatment on his arm.

CHAPTER TWENTY-ONE

SUMMING UP

Just over a week had passed since the ordeal in the churchyard. Morgan made a call on Pringle at his Sussex home. Pringle's wife admitted him and he followed her through to their back room where the injured detective sat taking it easy in an armchair. Pringle attempted to rise in politeness to his visitor but Morgan waved him not to do so.

'How are you feeling, old boy?' Morgan asked earnestly, casting an eye as he did so over the heavily bandaged arm in a sling.

'Fine,' the other said bravely. 'Thanks for taking the trouble to come and see me.' He indicated the chair opposite and Morgan sat down.

'I couldn't help noticing that card in a frame,' said Morgan.

'Oh, that one. I know it off by heart: *Never question your wife's choice... Look who she married!* We got that in the printing section at Amberley Museum and Heritage Centre; she's quite chuffed with that.'

'Well now,' Morgan said. 'It's over. Our part's done, except for one line of thought that I'll talk about as we go along. Now it's up to the Crown Prosecution to decide what charges are to be brought. At the very least, desecrating a grave, illegal drug trafficking and assault can be proven without any doubts of failure. As you pointed out earlier, the scourge of drugs is recognised as one of the most serious. Alleged to be related to practically most types of crime. We must continue to come down hard on the suppliers and peddlers that spread human misery and degradation,' he ended passionately.

Pringle moved his bad arm and flinched. 'It's all to do with money and resources nowadays,' he said with conviction.

Morgan glared across at him in fatherly fashion. 'If justice had to be measured by what could be afforded, it would be unacceptable.'

'Will there be enough evidence to make any charges of murder stick?'

'They should have enough for the brother using what we have uncovered. Brought about by our pretence that forced her hand to remove the last batch of drugs from its hiding place, subsequently revealing herself. I can understand from her point of view the risk of losing such a haul. Heroin and cocaine, with a street value of hundreds of thousands of pounds on the open market, is some incentive, eh?'

'Agreed, especially when you openly admitted finding somewhere in the region of double that value, rubbing salt in the wounds,' Pringle sighted cheerfully.

'As I've known all along, Constance York's murder would be near on impossible to pin on anyone because of the way it was done. But we now have the link of association with both the Yorks. In the case of Henry, I believe the homemade metal cosh that nearly broke your arm in two was the same weapon that killed him, but that has yet to be proven in a court of law. It is, however, likely to be compatible with the head injury. Another fact on the positive side is that since we have a definite suspect for murder, her and her husband's cars will be gone over by forensics with a fine-toothed comb for hair, clothing fibre and any other samples they look for. If there's evidence of Henry being in one of the cars, then that would naturally strengthen the case. Until then, we move on with the next conundrum the criminals and the powers that be throw at us.' Morgan paused to rub his eye.

'There's so much circumstantial evidence, but there's also much that is unclear to me,' Pringle admitted blandly.

Morgan gently nodded, understanding. 'We've done a lot more background checking since arresting Elizabeth Fairfield. In the interview room, she was back to her amiable self. You wouldn't think it's the same woman. She admitted to knowing both the Yorks – have it on tape; with the proof we had, she couldn't do otherwise. She also let slip, "stupid little diary being thumbed through; I wish I'd never met up with her again." But, as you know, on its own that is not enough; it must be backed up by undisputable evidence. I fully believe she will be found guilty of at least Henry's murder.'

'Is it possible to fit together most of what took place that led to the deaths of the Yorks?'

'Without a crystal ball, it's difficult to dot every "i" and cross every "t". I have a feeling in the end she may well make a full admission, as more and more of the facts are put to her. Events began, as I see it, on the day Constance York's main passion took her to a store to browse around the wine bottles on the shelves. She must have done that loads of times. If fate hadn't intervened by her striking up a conversation in that shop, events would have been entirely different. Both she and her brother would be alive today. What's frightening is that fate can deal any of us the same hand: a chance meeting that alters our destiny forever.'

'For a start, we would never have met,' Pringle observed thoughtfully.

'Probably not,' Morgan agreed. 'In this shop, the person that made her acquaintance told her about a friendly circle of men and women who meet and talk wine, are able to pick up tips, learn about all manner of interesting paraphernalia of wine production etcetera. What she hears pleases her. They are able to taste many types without buying full bottles that they would normally have to spend on and which would be wasted if not to their liking.'

'That's a very good idea for those interested in wine,' Pringle said.

'Constance goes along to the meeting. The one on the twentieth of July. She, in all probability, completely enjoys herself. Who should be there that evening giving the talk but Donald Fairfield? He had brought along for company brother Phillip and wife. His sister Pamela also goes. Donald Fairfield takes a few bottles of Châteaux La Rochelle. Constance has in the course of the evening been given a tasting of many wines and this one takes her fancy enough for her to purchase one or two. I wondered where I had seen one similar before. I'd seen it in the official shots taken in Constance's flat. What relevance is a bottle of wine in a home environment? None. Just backs up what I'm saying. It's what happened after the meeting broke up that proved significant. She'd left one of her gloves, hadn't she? And returned, we know that. All I've said so far can be checked out one way or another. Constance meets Liz in the street. They briefly talk as Constance is on her way back to retrieve her glove. Liz may have asked where she was working or living. Constance carries on but looks back to see who Liz is meeting, surprised no doubt that she is meeting Donald.'

Pringle's eyebrows rose. 'You leave me with so many questions.'

141

'You are thinking, how did they know one another? I'll come on to that. Constance, with knowledge of Liz's sordid past, resented her undeserved good fortune, and it was she who made the call to Lord P. She knew of Donald Fairfield's father being a lord from the presentation and the introduction delivered at the meeting by Mrs Morrison. Now... was the phone call just to warn of what type of woman his son was involved with, or was money the aim? He didn't listen. Whatever the motive, Liz Fairfield gets to hear of the call from family tittle-tattle. She knows who had recognised her that night and briefly spoken to her. She concocts a brilliant scheme in her mind. She gets in touch and they arrange a meeting. Options for the meeting could have included Constance's own flat. That might have involved a certain amount of risk being seen and later identified. In one of Constance's lunch breaks, at some café or restaurant, maybe. After that meeting, Constance York stayed out overnight and thus the need to take her bottle of capsules with her. Liz knew of Constance's allergy. My view is that Liz told Constance of her husband being away on business for a couple of days and, as a logical explanation, possibly invited her to a girls' night out. They could have stayed at Liz's home or some hotel. The hotel is the line of thought I spoke of earlier. It's a bit late; maybe this could be checked out. I believe Constance accepted the invitation and Liz, without mentioning what was on her mind, offered to help her with some money, fully knowing that by the time whatever was agreed upon was to change hands, Constance would be dead. There was the unexpected phone call at her place of work not long before she died. So many things to focus on. If I'm anywhere near the mark, Liz could only have put the poison capsule in the bottle on the morning they parted. Constance mustn't die until Liz was far away.' Morgan stopped; he thought Pringle was about to

142

say something, but he remained silent and Morgan pressed on. 'Constance apparently had no fear or premonition of how ruthless her old acquaintance could be. Somewhere along the line, Constance is nosey enough to poke around in Liz's diary and copy down those three names and places, and later adding to the list the Fairfield name. According to Constance's husband and others, she had a tendency to be over inquisitive.'

Pringle nodded.

'Donald Fairfield was away from his home on the night of the thirty-first of July, which matches with what Constance York's cleaning lady had to say about an undisturbed bed and no dirty breakfast things to attend to. The date is worth noting. Donald Fairfield has confirmed being in France and admitted not mentioning his wife meeting him outside the wine club that night.'

'Why on earth didn't he?'

'He felt it was of no significance – reasoned by his own pomposity. He's living in a world of his own.'

'Vital point,' Pringle said quickly, without letting Morgan continue. 'Fill me in on Constance York having known Liz Fairfield in the past.'

'You may recall me commenting on how far back the police should go into a victim's past. In this case it would have been wise to have gone back to her late schooldays, when she was in her teens. But even that would not have helped alone. It was only when we knew of Liz Fairfield's involvement and checked her maiden name that we discovered Elizabeth Makeland – as she was then – attended the same school as both Henry and Constance York.'

'Blimey!' Pringle said, astounded.

Morgan went on, 'The Makeland girl knocked about with a shifty character. Both were pushing drugs at school. There was quite a stir at that time and the police were called. A teenager died as the result of an overdose. This lad Makeland was associating with – by the name of Bobby Tamling – was caught in Newhaven, trying to bring more controlled drugs into this country. They were concealed in a false compartment on a petrol tank. He is now serving a prison sentence at Her Majesty's pleasure. One of the customs officers owned a car similar to the one this Bobby Tamling was driving, and noticed a big difference in the size of the tank underneath.

'Now you can see how all this is adding up. They must have met up again. She'd had enough of her husband's attitude towards her and being taken for granted. She began to despise him. Bobby Tamling had come up in the world and progressed with the hard drugs, and, until he was caught, was making a success of it. I don't know who thought of it, but the graves were a kind of safe hiding place until the drugs were required, and Liz was only too pleased to help. They may have made plans to go away together when convenient and in the money. As it was, things went wrong; he's caught and put inside. She coped nicely until the Yorks turn up one after the other. Liz having seen both of them off, I come along, having found two of their valuable assets. All of a sudden her dreams begin to crumble. There is only one batch remaining, and that is in danger of being found. She must salvage what still is a vast sum of money. That's why she did what she did, and why she is under lock and key. Do you recollect what Donald Fairfield said happened to him? About answering the phone a few times, and the one on the other end of the line never spoke a word, and put the receiver down each time?'

'Yes, I recall you telling me.'

'I believe it was Bobby Tamling. He was trying to contact Liz, but when Donald answered the phone, he dared not speak. Tamling had to rule out that way of getting in touch; it was too risky.'

'How do you know that?'

'It has been verified at the prison that Tamling made calls – as is his right. It has also been established that Liz Fairfield made two visits to Bobby Tamling in prison. And, as confirmation, her maiden name of Elizabeth Makeland was written down in the prison visitors' book.'

Pringle said enthusiastically, 'That ties up nicely – excellent. And Henry York, what can be summed up of him?'

'Without his fatal participation in all this, I believe I'd have got nowhere, and the death of Constance York would still be an unsolved. The list and other jottings his sister had were found by him. He comes to England and writes to the Yard to get our investigation started again, because at this stage he has nothing concrete to go on. He's unsure whether we'll take any notice. The name of Donald Fairfield, given him by Mrs Morrison, must have whetted his appetite. Most probably phoned to Donald's home address. He's hardly there, and Liz was on the other end. They arranged to meet. He came out with the names he had over the phone. Continuing along these lines, they met; she may even have enticed him into the woods with her. Him believing his luck had changed. She's strikingly attractive in a strange sort of way. He walks on in front of her; she brutally hits him on the back of the head and drags him to where he was found. Don't forget she has the cosh and small spade.'

Morgan paused briefly, then continued. 'Although her husband was away on the continent, she didn't have all the time in the world to make decisions. Such a quiet, timid woman on the surface, but obviously one with an unruly split personality and capable of murder when threatened.'

'With the parts she admitted to taped at the interview, is that going to be enough?'

'That's one of the drawbacks of police work, as well you know. They are feasible, but I'll stick to facts when I'm called to the stand in court – as will you. Present the evidence alone, let the jury make from it what they will; that's what they're there for. And of course there is the forensic evidence, and how good the prosecution. We are not barristers or forensic specialists. Many of the things I've said will come to light with good cross-examination during the trial.'

'That unidentified fingerprint in Constance York's bedroom at her flat had nothing whatsoever to do with this case.'

Morgan looked at Pringle's probing face thoughtfully. 'That print – extra line of work for us, of course – not relevant, but not all in life is in black and white. As you say, nothing to do with this case, but at other times criminals have cottoned on to the idea of collecting a cigarette end from outside a pub or a hair off the coat of a stranger or the like, and leaving it at their own crime scene, leading the police on a wild goose chase with the DNA of an innocent person. Just because you find something of someone at the scene of crime, doesn't mean he or she's done any wrongdoing. Ships that pass in the night,' he announced with a smile.

CHAPTER TWENTY-TWO

THE TRIAL

At the trial of Elizabeth Fairfield, there was enough solid evidence to add the further charge of the murder of Henry York. Not everything, but much of what Morgan had rationalised with Pringle turned out to be accurate. The cross-examination proved effective by pressing home the point of her strong association and overwhelming connecting events with the two victims. It all proved too much for her in the end, and Elizabeth Fairfield reluctantly confessed to both murders. She was on the verge of tears when she told the prosecutor, 'When I heard of the phone call to my father-in-law on the twenty-second of July, I realised that it was Constance York that had made it, and that she had to be stopped from revealing parts of my life I never wanted to be brought out in the open. I just couldn't let that happen.'

A few days after the trial, the phone rang in Lord Peter Fairfield's study; he picked up the receiver. A voice said, 'Please don't hang up on me like the last time. I'm not making any threats or demands. There will be no harm in listening to what I have to say.'

'I'm listening,' he said, astounded and uncomfortable.

'I've been reading the newspapers and I feel partly responsible for the unnecessary deaths of two people. Your daughter-in-law firmly believed Constance York made that call to you that put her on the pathway to murder, but it was not her who phoned; it was me, an illegitimate daughter of yours from one of your flings. I found this out from my mother's bundle of papers and an old diary, stored in the attic when we were clearing out her house before putting it up for sale. I was shocked and upset after I read the things she'd written. She passed peacefully away after a long illness. You may or may not remember the name of Brenda – I very much doubt that will mean anything at all to you. I was in two minds whether or not to ring you when I found out who my real father was. I should have let sleeping dogs lie. I had no intention of ringing again after that first call – until now. I must confess that curiosity got the better of me once and I waited outside your home in my car and got a glimpse of you. What's done is done. I can't turn the clock back – no more than you can. I will never phone you or make contact again.' She hung up on him before he could take in, or question, all she had said.

www.ingramcontent.com/pod-product-compliance
Lightning Source LLC
Chambersburg PA
CBHW060422260626
47161CB00005B/1741